DO949674

WITHDRAWN

Praise for
THE CASKET OF TIME

**Winner of the Icelandic Literary Prize
for Children and Young People's Books**

**Winner of the Icelandic Booksellers Prize
for Best Teenage Book of the Year**

**Nominated for the Nordic Council Children
and Young People's Literature Prize**

Winner of the West Nordic Literature Prize

Winner of the Reykjavik Children's Literature Prize

"The story confronts the concept of time and twists old fairy-tale memories with a passionate creativity."

**The Nordic Council Children and
Young People's Literature Prize Citation**

"The largest box of chocolates written in the Icelandic language that I have ever laid my hands on . . . This is confectionery for the mind! . . . This is a book for the 3-year-old, the 30-year-old, the 300-year-old."

**Audur Haraldsdóttir,
Channel 2, National Radio (Iceland)**

"The power of story animates a tale that communicates—but is not overpowered by—urgent messages."

Kirkus Reviews

"Andri Snær Magnason has created an intimate epic that floats effortlessly between genres as diverse as fairy tale and political commentary, science fiction and social realism. *The Casket of Time* spans the chasm between 'once upon a time' and 'have you heard the news today' in a way that makes his philosophical fable feel both timely and timeless."

Bjarke Ingels, architect

THE CASKET
OF TIME

THE CASKET OF TIME

Andri Snær Magnason

Translated from the Icelandic by
BJÖRG ÁRNADÓTTIR AND ANDREW CAUTHERY

Restless Books
for Young Readers

Title of the original Icelandic edition: *Tímakistan*
Published by agreement with Forlagið, www.forlagid.is

This book has been translated with a financial support from:

This book has been published with the assistance of the Sharjah International Book Fair Translation Fund.

This project is supported in part by the National Endowment for the Arts.

This book is made possible by the New York State Council on the Arts with the support of Governor Andrew M. Cuomo and the New York State Legislature.

First Restless Books hardcover edition April 2019

Hardcover ISBN: 9781632062055
Library of Congress Control Number: 2018956654
Cover design by Rachael Wilson
Cover artwork and lettering by Katla Rós and Ragnar Már
Set in Carré Noir by Tetragon, London
Printed in Canada

10 9 8 7 6 5 4 3 2 1

Restless Books, Inc.
232 3rd Street, Suite A111
Brooklyn, NY 11215

www.restlessbooks.org
publisher@restlessbooks.org

MIX
Paper from
responsible sources
FSC® C004071

And Time burns
its former wings
casts off the bonds
it was cursed to wear

flies out of the fire
toward blue forests
and each new spring
the trees burst into leaf

FROM
MJALLHVÍTARKISTAN
BY JÓN ÚR VÖR

THE CASKET
OF TIME

No More Februarys

It was a bright summer's day and the birds were singing, but no one seemed to be happy. The nation was in the grip of a "situation." Sigrun's parents talked of nothing else, hardly glancing up from their newspapers and computers, and the news channels were filled with economists and politicians arguing. Sigrun had become thoroughly fed up with the "situation," but she finally managed to drag her parents away from their screens to go buy ice cream and popcorn so they could settle down together at home to watch a comedy show.

On their way to the store they met a man with a sign that read: THE END IS NIGH!

"Is that an economist?" Sigrun asked.

"Shush!" said her mother. "Don't be silly, child. Economists wear suits."

When they got back home, Sigrun made the popcorn and took it to her parents in the den.

"Well, isn't this nice?" said her dad, making himself comfortable as they snuggled up on the couch.

The show started, and they forgot everything else and laughed at it for several minutes—until there was a sudden break.

"We are interrupting this transmission because of the situation," the announcer said.

Three economists appeared on the screen. *Oh no*, thought Sigrun. *Not again.* They looked like a three-headed giant.

"Are there such things as conjoined triplets?" she asked.

"Shush!" her mother said. "Don't be silly, we have to listen to this."

In a pained voice, one of the economists began to speak: "They say that reports have no feelings, but I swear mine wept when I calculated the situation for the year ahead." Her parents froze, horrified. Sigrun glared at the bowl of popcorn; losing patience, she grabbed the remote control and changed the channel.

"NO!" her father yelled. "This is important!" But they didn't miss anything. The economists were on the next channel, too, and the one after that. Sigrun snatched the bowl and went out into the yard.

The evening sun was shining, and the birds were singing. She sat down on the grass and breathed its freshly cut smell, but there was nobody else out enjoying the lovely weather; all their neighbors were transfixed by the gloom and doom on television. Through the window Sigrun eyed her parents, sitting there in the living room. She had finally set up some cozy family time, but this "situation" had once again ruined everything. On the TV, the economists were replaced by a commercial. Sigrun couldn't hear anything from where she was, but she saw three black boxes dancing on the screen, with the caption: Take control of your time! You only live once! Buy a TimeBox®!

Suddenly the front door burst open and her dad sprinted out and jumped into his car.

"Where are you going?" Sigrun called after him.

"You'll see," he said. "We've decided to wait until the situation has cleared up!"

Sigrun saw her next-door neighbor also dashing out to her car, and a man farther down the street doing the same.

A short time later, her dad returned carrying a set of large boards covered in Bubble Wrap. Her mom watched closely as he removed the wrapping, grabbed an Allen wrench, and started assembling three black boxes on the living-room floor. Sigrun kept half an eye on what was going on, amusing herself by popping the plastic bubbles.

"We're not going to put up with this crisis," her dad muttered. "The world cruise will have to wait." He looked sadly at a picture of a sailboat hanging on the wall, and her mother sighed grumpily.

"Yes, too right, life won't be worth living if this half-point reduction in the national index is for real," she said.

"What happens then?" Sigrun asked anxiously.

"Aside from the economists, nobody really knows," her mother said, "but you can bet it will be bad. A total nightmare."

Though Sigrun's father was considered solution-focused and innovative by his business colleagues, he was not much of a handyman. He usually sat all day in front of a computer, so he looked pretty pleased with himself when the black boxes finally stood on the living-room floor, all screwed together and looking like tall, slim refrigerators made of some kind of dark, tinted glass. He set them up in their bedrooms while her mother tidied the house, secured anything that was loose in the yard, backed the car into the garage, and put any food that might go moldy into the freezer. She arranged for the online bank to pay all bills automatically for a whole year in advance, and put a new message on the voicemail:

This is a message from the family at 22 Margo Court.
We have decided to wait for better times.
Please ring later.

"'I'll see you again, whenever spring breaks through again'," she sang.

"When will we come out of the boxes?" Sigrun asked.

"We've set them to 'Indexation.' They'll open automatically when the stock markets recover."

Sigrun looked around. Everything had been meticulously prepared, as if they were going on a long trip. One by one they now stepped into their black boxes—Mom, Dad, and Sigrun. Sigrun was full of curiosity as she entered her box; the glass was translucent, her ears popped when the door closed, and a blue light came on. For a moment everything went black, but then the box opened again. She stepped gingerly out into the hallway. She got goose bumps when she felt how damp the floor was; she went into the living room and was startled as a flock of black-headed gulls burst into flight. A small deer lying on the couch jumped up and leaped out the broken window. In the middle of the room a magnificent spruce had rooted through the parquet, and in the corner ferns had colonized the floor. A crow cawed. Sigrun looked up at the ceiling and saw blue sky through a hole in the roof. The crow flew off, a large spider in its beak.

By the time Sigrun reached the kitchen, she didn't bat an eye when she saw a squirrel sitting in the sink. It bolted through the broken window—the trees in the yard had advanced all the way to the wall of the house, and a branch had broken through the glass pane. The cupboards were open, and a swallow had made its nest in her favorite bowl.

Oh no, the economists were right, this is a terrible situation, Sigrun thought as she tried not to disturb the little nestlings chirping in the cupboard.

Her box must have malfunctioned. Sigrun tried to move quickly, because they were not supposed to come out until the crisis was over. She cleared the creeping plants away and saw that the family pictures on the wall had faded. She struggled through a blanket of ferns that had grown in front of her parent's room and pushed hard to get the door open. When her eyes had gotten used to the semidarkness, she saw them standing in their boxes, looking pale and ghostly in the bluish light. Her dad seemed to be saying something, and her mom's eyes were half-closed like in a bad photo. Sigrun wanted to tell her mom that her box had opened for some reason; she pulled hard on the handle and pushed with her foot. Nothing happened. She tapped on the glass. Her parents' expressions remained as rigid as ever, so she knocked as hard as she could. Still no reaction.

"MOM! MOM!" Sigrun yelled. She began to tear up but stopped herself and tried to think logically.

An Allen wrench! I need an Allen wrench! she thought and returned to the living room. "There must be one here some-where," she said aloud as she struggled to open the door that led through to the garage.

Suddenly she heard a shrill voice behind her: "Don't go in there! It's full of bees!" She looked round and saw a boy standing in the yard. He wore an old-fashioned dark brown woolen sweater and blue sweatpants with a hole in one knee.

"Who are you?" she asked.

"Marcus," the boy said. "You have to come with me."

Sigrun looked at him.

"Do you have an Allen wrench?" she said.

"What?"

"I need to find an Allen wrench. You know, like a bent piece of metal with a hexagon at one end."

"No," said the boy. "An Allen wrench won't fix anything. Come on, hurry. The front door is jammed; you'll have to come through the window. You'd better grab a coat and some shoes."

7

The lower part of the split-level living room was flooded, half-full of murky water. A frog sat on the coffee table, floating in a kind of pond.

"I can't reach it," Sigrun said. "There's a frog on the coffee table."

"Just step on things."

Using chairs as stepping-stones, Sigrun navigated across the room and climbed out the broken window. The yard was overgrown with yellow, withered grass.

"Is there still a situation?" she asked, looking around. She hardly recognized her neighborhood; the forest seemed to have swallowed it.

"A lot worse than that," said the boy.

They headed off down the road—except that, with large poplar trees growing in the middle, it was hardly a road anymore. The city seemed to be under a spell. The houses were gray and weathered, the paint flaking or worn away, and ivy stretched up their walls. It was as if all the people had disappeared; it was as if the world was abandoned.

There were weird-looking signs posted on mailboxes and front doors:

MISERABLE MONDAY!

Near the intersection was a rotating billboard with the slogan:

DID YOU SUCCEED TODAY?
A WASTED DAY IS GONE FOREVER!
TimeBox®

The road was lined with large mossy mounds.

"Are those cars? They look like hedgehogs! What happened? Where are all the people?"

"Hush," said Marcus, "we must be careful. Hurry up." Sigrun followed Marcus along an abandoned highway until they reached the river that flowed through a green valley in the center of town. They followed the river toward the suburbs. On one side of the valley were tall apartment buildings, but Marcus led them away toward some faded, detached homes up on the other side. They threaded their way through the yards, until a boy wearing a bright-colored hoodie called out to them and signaled for them to come into one of the houses.

Sigrun stepped inside. The walls of the high-ceilinged lobby were lined with works of art and antiques; there was a row of pillars topped with human heads sculpted from marble, their staring eyes made of black pearls. They entered a room, to find a motley collection of children who seemed to be from different lands and of different ages. The large parlor windows gave a view across the whole city, but there was no sign of life out there. Not one single human being. On the side of an apartment block beyond the river, an enormous sign blinked:

NO MORE FEBRUARYS!

Sigrun was completely baffled. An elderly woman appeared. She had a long, gray braid and wore a black dress. She smiled at Marcus, and then came straight over to Sigrun and greeted her kindly.

"Welcome, my dear, my name is Grace. Do sit down with the other children."

She went to the kitchen and returned with a plate of freshly baked cinnamon rolls. Sigrun watched her with suspicion. She was beginning to understand that this was not a dream. The city really was in ruins. Everybody really had vanished. She glanced toward the open door where the boy in the hoodie remained, seemingly on guard.

One of the children, a fair-haired girl, began to sob. "I want to go home," she cried.

Grace addressed her gently: "Don't cry, my dear. It will be alright. If everything goes well, you'll be able to go home soon."

"Where's my little sister? Where did all the people go?"

"To find the answer to that I need you all to help me," Grace said.

Sigrun gazed out the window—at the leaves that were blowing along the streets, at the faded signs, at the totally desolate world—and felt exactly the same.

Grace picked up a pair of binoculars and looked out over the city.

"We'll have to wait for the others." She put down the binoculars and returned to the kitchen.

Sigrun snuck over to the window and picked up the binoculars. There must be somebody at home, somewhere in the whole city. In one of the houses she spotted a blue light that looked like the flickering glow of a television. She focused in that direction. On the front door of the house was a sticker with a smiley face:

BETTER TIMES AROUND THE CORNER!

She looked through the window into the living room. There were faded flowers on the sill and she could see glasses on tables and sofas covered with gray dust. It looked as if the apartment had been abandoned in a great hurry. She searched for the blue glow and found a woman in a box, her face transfixed like a waxwork;

10

there too were her husband and their child, just as frozen. This wasn't a family watching television she was looking at, it was a set of petrified faces.

She put the binoculars down and saw a girl running along the road, the coat over her shoulders making it look as if she had blue wings. She fluttered toward the house like a moth seeking a porch light, turning now and then to call to a boy following her.

"There's a girl out there," Sigrun called out. "She's heading this way."

Marcus looked out. "It's Kristin. She's found someone!"

"Tell her to hurry up," said Grace. "Dusk is falling, and the wolves might be on the prowl."

The girl with the coat appeared in the doorway, followed by a boy who looked as confused as Sigrun felt.

"Come in and have some cocoa," said Grace. "Something's happened to the world, but we're going to fix it."

"Any more kids coming?" said Marcus.

"No," said Kristin. Catching her breath, she took off her coat. "I didn't see any others."

"Where am I?" asked the new boy. "Where are all the people? There's nobody out there!"

"It's polite to introduce yourself," Grace said.

"I'm Peter Wilson."

"Welcome, Peter. No need to be afraid."

Sigrun looked at the old woman and her elegant hands. She looked at the furniture, the rug on the floor and the lights hanging from the ceiling. With its paintings, and shelves laden with books and scientific instruments, it wasn't so much a home as a combination of art gallery, library, and laboratory. She shook her head when the old woman offered her a slice of chocolate cake and a glass of milk; she was all too familiar with the story of Hansel and Gretel.

"Come with me," Grace said. The children followed her into an office. There was an ancient clay pot on a pillar, and on a shelf sat a helmet split in two as if somebody had slashed it with a sword. They saw remnants of an old rug hanging on a wall, and a recent drawing of an enormous ancient castle. There was a scabbard, a silver ring, a small carved elephant, and a narwhal tusk. There were ancient maps showing the world as people imagined it in previous times, with places marked on them in felt-tip pen. Stuck to the map of the world was a yellow Post-it note with the words: The Curse of the Princess of Pangea.

Grace pulled back a drape to reveal a large painting, somewhat fragmentary but colorful and artistically drawn. It showed a man who was obviously a king leading a rhinoceros in harness; a girl carrying a gigantic goldfish, with a boy guiding her toward a little lake; and the same girl lying in something that looked like a glass casket.

"Who's the girl in the box?" Sigrun asked.

"That's Obsidiana, the princess of Pangea," Grace said. "I've collected thousands of stories about her and studied how they relate to what's happened here; I've excavated relics and ruins, and I'm close to a solution. I think I've found the only way to free the world from a curse, but you all have to help me."

Grace played them a video clip of a man standing in a deserted city pointing at a hill behind him. He shook his head and said in a somber voice: "Somebody must have disturbed her! The curse has been revived!"

The children sat transfixed. Outside all was still; there was not a soul to be seen and no lights in the city save for the pale blue glow emanating from its silent homes. The flat screen on the wall showed webcam clips from all over the world. Everywhere it was the same story: ghost houses, ghost avenues, ghost towns. Everything was abandoned and empty, but the world was far from dead—it was green and luxuriant, its sidewalks and concrete hidden by forests. The world had surely been put under some kind of spell.

Grace picked up a bunch of papers and thumped it onto the table, startling the children.

"Would you like to hear the story?" The children nodded. Grace began.

The Three Sisters

A long, long time ago, when humans were few and roamed the land as hunter-gatherers, three sisters were born.

Their mother quickly saw that one was blind and deaf, and could only talk; one was blind and mute, and could only hear; one was deaf and mute, and could only see.

The sisters grew up, each making up for what the others lacked. The sister who could hear had super-sensitive hearing, the sister who could see had eyes sharper than an eagle's, and the talking sister could shout so loud that wild beasts took flight. And so together they roamed the forest and knew their way better than anyone with perfect sight and hearing.

The people, however, were scared of the sisters and thought they would bring bad luck. Their mother was forced to abandon them in a clearing and leave them to die.

But the wildest of beasts didn't harm them. The seeing one would gaze deep into the animals' eyes, the hearing one listened compassionately to them, the one who spoke stroked them and whispered kind words to them.

Cows came and gave them milk, horses carried them across mountains, and wolves brought them rabbits and pheasants to eat. They found shelter in a gigantic hive that the bees built for them.

The people never knew when or where in the forest they might encounter the sisters. This so terrified them that they chose a brave young man to go kill the three of them and bring back their hearts as proof. The young man headed off and eventually found their beehive in a forest clearing. He hid under a fur, knife in hand. He saw a young girl come home, whispering to a small bird in the palm of her hand. He pricked up his ears and listened to the girl's rhymes. He lay stock-still all day and heard her whisper cow-rhymes and horse-rhymes and a rhyme that calmed the wolves' ferocity. No other human had ever communed so intimately with the animals.

He was still in hiding when the hearing sister returned. She stopped, hearing the throb of an unfamiliar heartbeat. She moved toward the sound, reached under the fur and pulled the young man out. The seeing sister looked fixedly into his eyes and gazed deep into his soul, and the sister who could only speak hissed in his ear: "You have learned rhymes that will make you powerful. But know this: you must never set animals against people. NEVER! Whosoever does this will lose what is dearest to him."

Terrified, the young man ran off, and for hours wandered around the forest in confusion, until he came across a stag. Instinctively he reached for his knife, but instead of attacking he whispered the stag-rhyme. And that was how it came about that he returned to his people sitting astride a stag instead of bringing back the hearts of the three sisters. The people knelt before him and made him their king. He tamed horses and cows and elephants and built a bigger palace than anyone had ever seen. He tamed camels and rode them across impassable deserts. This was how the first town came about, which then became the first city, which then became the first nation and was named Pangea. The young man had sons who succeeded to the throne, and centuries and yet more centuries passed.

From generation to generation, official whisperers served the kings of Pangea, and though the kings may not all have been peaceful rulers, none dared to set animals against people.

For ages nothing was heard of the sisters, but legend had it that they would sometimes appear and augur bad tidings. And now it came about that there were sightings in Pangea of all three of them: one on a mountain top at full moon, another close by a fisherman hauling in his nets, and another sitting in a crow's nest.

But King Dimon the Thirteenth never heard about the sightings. For he was in love—completely and utterly in love.

Life and Death

King Dimon of Pangea had been remarkably absent-minded of late. Counselors and courtiers would find him staring dreamily into space, and everybody knew why. While out hunting in the forest, Dimon had met a wondrously beautiful woman fishing for trout in a little lake. A mighty tiger stretched languidly by her feet.

He greeted her, and she greeted him and said her name was Sunbeam.

Her eyes were as dreamy as a hovering jellyfish, her hair rippled like seaweed on the shore, and her lips were as red as a starfish.

"Starfish," Dimon thought. "Starfish." His heart was wriggling like a newborn dolphin.

Together they swam out to a small island in the lake, where they sat all day beneath an old whitebeam tree, chatting and chewing on straws. By evening he was so overwhelmed with love that he asked her to move into the castle with him.

"I would rather you stayed with me," she said with a teasing smile.

"But who will rule my kingdom?"

"Sometimes one can rule more by ruling less," she said as she landed a thrashing trout.

Back in his castle, this was exactly what the king decided to do. At the first opportunity he leaped astride his horse and rode into the forest.

"I'll see you in the fall!" he shouted to Consiglio, his counselor. "But who is going to rule?"

"Sometimes one can rule more by ruling less," Dimon replied, and disappeared.

Dimon and Sunbeam spent the whole summer together in a cottage by the little lake and could be heard giggling and laughing well into the night. He told her of his dream to extend his realm, but she just wrapped her arms around him and said:

"Come now, all we need is a single grove, a few tussocks, and a pond."

As time went on, a new little life was kindled in her belly, and to the king the world seemed like the sweetest sugar and every sound like birdsong.

They had a grand wedding, with cheering crowds and thousands of birds creating a vivid display that looked like fireworks in the sky.

When the child was ready to enter the world, Sunbeam was taken up to a tower room in the palace and laid in a silken bed, with a view across mountains and valleys where parrots flew from tree to tree. But the birth turned out to be difficult. A day and a night passed before the child at last came into the world and a call went out from the tower: "A GIRL IS BORN!"

The queen took the baby into her arms, gave a faint smile and said: "How beautiful she is."

Then she closed her eyes, never to open them again. The midwife took the child from her, while the king tried to rouse his one and only love; but she did not wake.

King Dimon buried his face in his hands. His heart shattered into a million pieces. This couldn't be true! Only a moment ago the love of his life had kissed him, but now she was gone forever.

It was as if a little star in his breast had imploded and turned into a black hole that sucked in all the joy he possessed. He gazed at the horizon, at the sun and the wind and the world that carried on as if nothing at all had happened. The flies went on buzzing, the birds chirruped merrily, and the sun shone as if it was the most natural thing in the world.

Dimon yelled with all his might: "STOP SINGING! I ORDER YOU TO STOP SINGING! TO HELL WITH YOU ALL!"

Suddenly he heard soft, delicate whimpering, so gentle and vulnerable that the beat of his heart changed immediately. He took his newborn daughter into his arms to stop her crying. He was clumsy, and his big hands had never held such a tiny life. He kissed her forehead. She smelled like a flower and gazed at her father with eyes like a seal's—inquisitive, deep, and intelligent. He laughed and cried at the same time, and then she began to cry again.

"She's hungry," said the midwife.

A messenger rushed from house to house looking for a woman who could nurse a baby. That was how they found Thordis; she had gentle hands, a beautiful smile, and golden hair. Thordis nursed the princess with love and lavished on the baby all the affection she needed.

Dimon seethed with anger and a sense of loss; fate had turned against him. That night, he took the dead queen in his arms and rode with her into the forest. He buried her by the little lake where they had spent the summer.

The news spread throughout the realm that the most beautiful girl had been born—white as snow, with lips as red as blood and hair as black as a raven's wing. Her father closed his eyes and said:

"I swear by all the gods that I will do everything for this child. I will climb mountains and win wars. All for her happiness." She was given the name Obsidiana.

Dimon carried her out onto the balcony so that the citizens could see their new crown princess. The people rejoiced, and poets wrote ballads. Nobody imagined that decades later she would stand on this same balcony and people would be looking up at her, their eyes full of terror.

Exel

Restless though he had been when lovestruck, in grief the king was much worse. In an attempt to comfort him and distract him from his pain, Consiglio suggested they go for a walk together. The counselor had trained a swarm of bees to fly around his head like Saturn's rings. He carried an old squirrel on his shoulder, and behind him a pair of black boa constrictors slithered around in his shadow, sometimes intertwining so they looked like a two-headed serpent.

Consiglio demonstrated to Dimon how everything prospered, how wonderful his kingdom was, better than any other in the world. Passing by the river they saw an otter climb onto the bank and bring a fish to a fisherman sleeping nearby. They saw a monkey climbing a tree to collect coconuts, which he stacked in a pile next to an old woman who sat knitting a hat. Nearby, a rust-colored rhinoceros was pulling a plow. The kingdom flourished, the barns were filled with hay, the storerooms were crammed with dried fish, and every jar was brimming with jam—but none of this consoled the king.

The old sage Jako descended into the depths of the library, desperately looking for some words of wisdom that could free the king from the chains of his sorrow. The royal chefs prepared the tastiest food for their monarch; they served a whole grilled ostrich stuffed with a great auk stuffed with a turkey stuffed with a flamingo stuffed with a chicken stuffed with a ptarmigan stuffed with a parrot stuffed with a meadow pipit stuffed with a hummingbird that had a honey-glazed bee in its bottom. But the king had no appetite. It was only when his little girl gurgled and pulled his nose that he briefly forgot his woes. Countless tasks awaited his attention, and back in those days it was not the custom for men of such importance to waste their precious time on children. It therefore fell to Thordis the nursemaid to take charge of that, aided by one hundred ladies-in-waiting.

"Does she have the world's best teachers?" demanded the king. "Has she studied singing and astronomy?"

"The child is still only a few months old," Consiglio said, "but we will get the very best teachers when she's older."

"Does she get the best food in the world?" asked the king.

"Thordis is still nursing her," said Consiglio, "but we will appoint the very best chefs when the time comes."

At night, grief completely consumed the king, and he roamed around the palace like a caged lion.

Dr. Stagg, the court physician, measured his heartbeat and asked, "What joy would suffice to ease your sorrow?"

The king said, "My sorrow is so deep that I would have to conquer the whole world."

"In that case there isn't much I can do for you," the doctor replied.

Just then a shrill voice piped up behind them, "I know how the world can be conquered."

The king turned around. Standing in the doorway was a tall, moldy-looking man so altogether gray that he merged into the walls of the castle. His suit was checkered like graph paper and he carried a silver-plated ruler. As he approached the king it became obvious he was taking care not to tread on any lines—because the floor tiles were of different sizes, every third step he took was either tiny or gigantic. He cleared his throat and said in a slightly high-pitched voice:

"I hope I do not disturb Your Majesty, but my name is Exel, and I think I can be of assistance to you."

"Where have you sprung from?" the king asked.

"I look after your accounts, Sire."

"Do you indeed?" The king was surprised; he couldn't remember having seen this man before. "Why would you know what it takes to conquer the world?"

"I have made some calculations," Exel said. "You will need immense quantities of gold, and I have found a way of changing air into gold."

The king arched his eyebrows and the court physician shook his head.

"Well," said the king, "what do you need in order to change air into gold?"

"I'll need an attic room and a large tray of haggis." The king had never heard anything so silly in his life, but his curiosity got the better of him and he arranged for Exel to have what he asked for.

The following day a bright beam of light shone through the keyhole of the attic room. When the king opened the door, he was dazzled—the room was filled with pieces of gold and sparkling diamonds. Exel sat proudly at his desk next to the glittering pile, weighing each item of treasure and recording it in a massive ledger.

"What did I tell you!" said Exel merrily, continuing to weigh. His face glowed in the glimmer from the gold.

"What's the secret of this magic?" the king asked.

"I taught the crows to bring me everything that glitters in exchange for a piece of haggis," said Exel triumphantly.

The king's eyes lit up as he contemplated all this treasure, and a tiny drop of sadness in his soul evaporated.

Consiglio looked doubtful. "We have never permitted crows to collect gold," he said.

"Don't worry," Exel said. "I have calculated everything. The rest will follow naturally."

It was not long before the rulers of neighboring states began to begrudge the king his gold, claiming that it came from their own treasuries. Together, the states formed a mighty army and laid siege to the city of Pangea.

"A hell of a mess you've got us into, Exel!" the king thundered.

But Exel was determined.

"Worry not, Sire. I have worked out that the smallest beast can conquer the largest army."

"How can that be?"

"Trust me."

"But Your Majesty," Consiglio protested. "We have never set beasts against humans."

The rhythmic marching of the enemy troops shook the palace and woke the baby princess, who started to cry.

"These forces are a threat to my child!" Dimon said. The city gates were barricaded while the king's men followed Exel's instructions, working day and night to train termites, bees, army ants, and many other tiny creatures. On the third day the bugs set upon the invaders, who scratched in panic as fleas jumped under their clothes. Termites gnawed through their arrows, pikestaffs, and shields, and moths chewed through their laces and uniforms, leaving them stark naked. Then the bees attacked. At dawn the enemy ranks stood there exposed and swollen from all the stings and bites. They raised a white flag, but it collapsed when termites gnawed through the pole.

"Well," said Dimon, chuckling over his easy victory. "What do you suggest? Shall we drive them away or kill them?"

"I suggest we give them the gold," said Exel.

"What!" The king was astounded.

"I've calculated the strengths, weaknesses, opportunities, and threats of the situation. I propose we buy the soldiers' allegiance and annex the states that attacked us."

All went as Exel had predicted. The enemy surrendered and received in compensation gold medals, weapons, and honor.

And so the army doubled in size and marched off to capture the next city, where the same method was employed. King Dimon's empire expanded like a forest fire in a westerly gale. The palace expanded, the kingdom flourished, and statues of Dimon were erected in places where his name had not been known before.

Dimon looked gleefully at the map and saw how mighty his realm had become.

"Now what?" he said.

"The smallest creatures have defeated huge armies," Exel replied, "but we will not conquer the whole world unless the large animals join the fray."

The king smiled, but Consiglio's face reddened. The bees sat on his bald head like a hat. "When the three sisters taught The Whispering to your ancestors, a promise was made never to set animals against people!" he said.

"Don't worry about old folk tales," the king said. "Where I conquer, goodness prevails."

The king issued a decree. Whisperers and tamers were given new rhymes to whisper to the animals. Arctic terns grouped together and practiced air raids; bulls snorted, pawing the ground and lowering their horns; rhinos grunted, armed for battle. Dimon surveyed his herds. They were clearly invincible—bellowing, snorting, growling, squealing, screaming, screeching, and cackling.

Birds of prey hovered in clouds above the castle. King Dimon waved his fist at the gods above:

"You think you rule the world, but I'll show you who is the greatest! Generals! Gather your troops! Harness the rhinos! Sharpen the bulls' horns! Water the horses! Hone the spears! Feed the lawyers! In the name of my daughter Obsidiana, I am going to conquer the world!"

And with that Dimon kissed the little princess goodbye and headed off with his army. He crossed the twelve mountains, traversed the four deserts, penetrated endless forests. He went farther than the nose could smell, farther than the ear could hear, farther than the eye could see, and even farther than the mind could imagine.

When all these creatures had left on their crusade, the city became curiously still and silent. The little princess was left behind at the palace with her nurse Thordis, one hundred ladies-in-waiting, and one thousand guards. The king had ordered that she should be the happiest child in the world. Exel was in charge of palace life, and his experts calculated exactly what would be the very best for the baby. Obsidiana was the sole heir, and without her all Dimon's conquests would be for nothing.

Obsidiana and the Pond

The earth trembled as King Dimon and his troops rode from region to region and from country to country. Ahead of their advance, birds scattered, wild beasts stampeded, and cities emptied as people fled to higher ground. Nowhere in the world was there a greater army. Never before had men set trained bees or armed rhinos against human foes. The rumbling and roaring were enough to make the fiercest fighters crumple with fear, and if the enemy did not surrender at once, the consequences were dire: Rhinos would cut through the front line, berserkers with snarling lions would rush in, and the cavalry, hacking right and left with their swords, would ride in and storm the hiding places of the kings and their noblemen. Hyenas and wolves were left in the ruins of towns and cities that still showed defiance.

After each encounter, King Dimon drove across the battlefield in a silver carriage drawn by a black horse, mighty as an ox, past huddles of injured and defeated soldiers, and past tall piles of the slain circled by vultures. He summoned kings and princes to his presence and offered them coffee and pastries while Consiglio opened his briefcase and said: "This is a statement in triplicate declaring surrender and everlasting loyalty to the King of Pangea. Sign here and here." Chroniclers toiled to send home fantastic descriptions of epic battles and great bravery.

*

The empire flourished. The people in the east called the king's palace Krabaduso Rundi, meaning "head of the octopus," because it seemed to have tentacles extending all over the world. In the west they called it The Vortex because from it all power issued and into it all wealth was sucked as if into a gigantic storm drain. The palace glowed in the heat of the sun, growing like a conch shell atop the hill overlooking the city of Pangea, and at its center was the fair princess Obsidiana, who sat at a window watching craftsmen decorate golden walls with black and white pearls. She watched as towers were built one on top of another, over and over until their highest pinnacles seemed to be touching the clouds and scraping at the stars.

The whole universe belonged to Obsidiana, but she longed only for the king's return. She looked at the great amphitheater and heard the distant sound of cheering and rejoicing. What were they cheering about? She gazed at the Seven Towers on the distant mountain peaks in the east. She yearned to go there. She peered over the battlements and wondered whether she could clamber down the castle wall, and if it would hurt if she fell. She had never injured herself—when King Dimon heard at the battlefront that she had begun to walk, he had issued a decree:

"Henceforth all sharp corners are prohibited anywhere in Pangea."

Dimon had the palace lined with rugs and silk cushions. Guards stood ready to catch Obsidiana wherever she might fall. As a small child she loved to run to the top of the stairs and have somebody catch her. She felt a rush in her tummy as she fell toward the hard stone floor and giggled as the guards caught her in a silk rug. They sighed with relief and wiped their sweaty brows because it wasn't just her life that was at stake, but also their own. Obsidiana was so well looked after that she hadn't so much as scratched her knee and had never found out what fun it is to pick the scab off a wound.

She scanned the horizon hoping to see a mail crow flying in with a note from her father. She hadn't seen any for several weeks. She had a huge pile of letters, which she had read time and time again:

> *My dearest daughter, following our latest triumph, you own a diamond castle in a city that now bears your name, Obsidiana City. We must visit it together when overall victory has been secured . . .*

Dimon's letters were full of awesome mountains, dark forests, and golden cities. He wrote of strange nations, wild animals, and forests full of cannibals. He told her of weird beasts, amazing fish, and great battles. Obsidiana closed her eyes and tried to remember her father. She tried to remember his eyes, his nose, and his voice. All she had were his letters. Her father had become nothing but a collection of words:

> *My dear daughter, we have now traveled the world for ten years and it is larger than I could have imagined. When I get back home, I will show you the grove where your mother rests beneath a weeping willow. Only I know where it is. It's in a lovely forest with a beautiful lake full of wriggling trout.*
> *I miss you – Papa*

A red panda jumped into Obsidiana's arms. She stroked it gently. The panda was the size of a raccoon and was rare and precious, like everything that Obsidiana owned.

She scratched the panda behind its ear, observing a scruffy dog as it jumped along the distant rooftops in the city. She wanted to stroke the dog, too.

"Wouldn't you like to play with a dog like that, my panda?" she whispered; the panda nuzzled her neck, tickling her with its whiskers.

Running with the dog was a child, whom Obsidiana longed to play with but knew this was unlikely to happen. She had seen hundreds of children standing in line to take the "friendship test." They came smartly dressed and with beautifully combed hair, only to walk sadly away a little later, the mother scolding them and the father striding on ahead. It was only a week ago that Exel presented his file and dryly announced the result:

"The inconceivable has happened yet again: Out of three thousand exceptional children who have taken the test, none has turned out to be Obsidiana's equal. Isn't that extraordinary?"

Everybody in the hall applauded except Obsidiana. She looked at him and asked:

"Does that mean that none of them can be my friend?"

"I'm afraid so, none of them passed the test," Exel replied.

"Can I take the test?" she asked.

"Why?" Exel asked, in surprise.

"Well, I need to know if I'm good enough for myself."

Exel laughed and said, "See how clever she is—what other child would have thought of a thing like that?"

Obsidiana decided to get back at him. She drew chalk lines all across the corridor on one of Exel's usual routes around the palace and lay in wait for him. When he saw the lines crisscrossing the hall, he came to an abrupt halt. Obsidiana darted past and chalked more lines behind him; he stood there as if frozen.

"Can't you tread on a line?" she teased.

Exel tried to step between the lines but gave up, cursing: "GUARDS! GUARDS! Clean the floor!"

"Aren't I clever? What other child would have thought of a thing like that?" Obsidiana said, laughing.

Exel shook with fear, but he didn't scold her. By royal command, nobody was allowed to scold the princess.

Obsidiana continued watching the dog and the child until they disappeared around a corner. Her nursemaid Thordis came to her and said amiably, "You're staring out the window."

"Yes," Obsidiana said. "I want to stroke a dog. I want to scrape my knee."

"What nonsense you speak!"

"I would like to have a friend."

"That isn't up to me, my dear. The children failed the friendship test. You'll have to speak to your father about that."

"When will he come home?"

"When he has conquered the world. Soon everything will be better, mark my words. Go talk to Jako, he'll have some words of wisdom for you."

Obsidiana wandered off, leaving Thordis to look wistfully out the window. Somewhere in the city was a child and a family that she had longed to see ever since that fateful night when she was summoned to receive the honor of becoming the royal nursemaid.

Obsidiana wandered along golden corridors and out into the palace gardens. This was where old Jako sat and looked after the goldfish and waterlilies in a small pond and tended to her animals. She had a miniature zoo, a tiny rhino the size of a cat and two elephants hardly bigger than puppies, but her favorites were Moon and Peak, two white deer that always came to her when she called. Servants and guards were not allowed to speak to her—they were not educated enough—but Jako could do so as long as he spoke in proverbs.

"Good day, Jako," she said.

"Good day, Obsidiana. All roads leading to a dear friend are good ones."

She sat down on the bank and the fish swam calmly toward her. Being well fed, some of the goldfish were the size of giant salamanders or small crocodiles.

"It's my birthday soon," Obsidiana said.

"Who lives well extols the years!"

"I'll be ten years old."

"Life begins at ten."

"Papa's going to send me more animals."

"Oh my! I hope he won't be sending a giraffe," said Jako, stroking his gray hair.

"Was that a proverb?" she said, teasingly. Jako scratched his head and thought it over.

"A tall giraffe will chew the chandeliers," he said, looking profound. "That's a proverb, is it not?"

"We'll have a party when Papa comes home," said Obsidiana somewhat listlessly. It was such a long time since his last visit.

Her little wood by the pond was surrounded by low stone walls. Tiny oak trees grew here, and miniature sequoias and cherry trees that hardly reached her knees. Their leaves were delicate and their trunks slim even though they were hundreds of years old. There was a dollhouse made of ivory, and toadstools so large that she could sit beneath them to shelter from rain or sun.

She strolled around the wood, whispering, "Moon! Peak! Where are you?" and rustling the grass in her pail to attract their attention. The white deer came running to her and she picked Moon up and patted him gently.

By royal command, nothing dangerous was to even come near the princess, and the guards were instructed to kill any bugs they saw. Obsidiana, however, always managed to find the occasional centipede, ladybug, or cockroach, which she would catch with an old jewelry box and hide in her little dollhouse. She told nobody about the bat that slept hanging beneath the roof of the garden shed—the last time she had pointed out a bat, a guard came and took it away in a bag. And she kept quiet about her friend the spider, who lived in the attic of the dollhouse and took up a whole room to spin its web. This was the spooky room, where she kept her naughty dolls. If she pulled off their wings, houseflies became black bears, bees became tigers, and black wasps became fierce wolves. One room she filled with cast-off jewelry, and here a small lizard was coiled up on a pile of old gold trinkets.

Nobody knew about this insect zoo until a guard found a wingless bee and removed it. A little later Thordis appeared and scolded her.

"But it was a tiger!" Obsidiana said.

"You aren't allowed to change a bee into a tiger!"

Obsidiana pouted and whimpered, "You're not my mom! If I wasn't here my mom would still be alive."

Thordis fell silent, her expression softened, and she hugged Obsidiana.

"You must never say such a thing! Nothing in the whole world can be blamed on a baby." She gazed deep into Obsidiana's eyes and said, "My dear little wish, I believe that your mother is somewhere, keeping an eye on you. When you laugh, she laughs too."

Thordis slipped a hand into her apron pocket and fished out a cake; Obsidiana wiped away her tears and nibbled at it. She looked at her necklace, the only keepsake she had from her mother, and said:

"I wish I had a mom." That pricked Thordis to the heart, because she had nursed Obsidiana; she had fed her and dressed her and read stories to her ever since the day she was born.

Obsidiana had grown. Stuck in the palace, she felt it was squeezing her, like a dress that had become too small and was bursting at the seams. She had to have friends. She had to go downtown and see the world. She could wait no longer. She peered out the window at the interminable walls. She had just begun to climb out onto the windowsill when she was startled by the arrival of a mail crow. The crow bowed and offered a sharp claw. Obsidiana whispered a tiny thank-you rhyme and undid the small slip of paper attached to the bird's leg.

My dearest daughter, I'm sending you this note from the remotest corner of the northern world. We have conquered the south and joined east and west together; all that remains is the extreme north. Soon we shall raise a flag on the roof of the world, where the compass needle points in all directions—toward the world I have conquered for you.

With all my love – Papa.

Obsidiana jumped her own height with joy and shouted: "Papa is coming home! He's coming home!" She ran along the palace corridors waving the letter. "Dad's coming home! Hurry, Thordis, let's prepare for his homecoming! We can celebrate all my birthdays at once!"

Thordis embraced her and smiled, and the ladies-in-waiting danced around them. Then Exel appeared with his file. Drily, he said:

"That is good news. After he has conquered the polar ice sheet, his journey home will only take two years."

Obsidiana's smile faded momentarily, but then she said:

"That doesn't matter—at least he's coming home!" She sat down at her window again and saw swans flying past in V-formation. She wished that a hundred swans could carry the king home on their white wings.

The Weird Woman
of the North

It would be a symbolic victory for Dimon to raise a flag on the world's northernmost place, where all directions meet at a single point. The frost bit hard and a freezing wind swirled the snow around, making it ripple across the earth like a white veil. "Your Majesty, do we have to take the whole army?" asked Consiglio, shivering as he tightened the fastenings of his squirrel-fur hat. "There's nothing there, maybe an old walrus at the very most."

But, shouting "Onward to the north!" Dimon urged his men on. Slowly they trudged, step by step, toward the goal. Their beards were caked with ice and the wind scoured their faces. Some could snap the tips of their noses off like icicles; their fingers and toes were blue with frostbite.

The route they had taken was lined with soldiers who had turned to ice as they lay in their tents. The soldiers stuck them into the snow at regular intervals, like frozen telephone poles, so that the victorious army would be sure to find its way back. Dimon was tired but proud when the compass needle at last began to spin around in circles.

An orange flag was attached to a pole, where it flapped like a flaming torch as proof that the world had been completely conquered. Dimon was moved, and tears froze at the corners of his eyes. The soldiers cheered, and their icy beards clinked like crystal glasses.

Suddenly they saw an old woman moving across the ice toward them, clad in a thick polar bear skin. She carried a staff made from the long, twisted tusk of a narwhal, jabbing it down and hopping like a kid over holes and cracks in the ice. She jabbed and hopped and jabbed and hopped as if she were stitching a pattern into a white cloth. She huffed and she puffed and chanted a strange spell as she stitched herself closer. With shaking hands, Consiglio fumbled in his briefcase to find a declaration for her to sign.

"You greedy king!" she hissed. "You've broken your promise! Broken your promise!"

She approached the king—she was so short and stooping that none of the guards felt there was any need to stop her—and thrust the point of her staff to his chest. She looked straight through him as if she were blind, and it seemed as though fire burned in her ice-blue eyes.

"Greedy king! You set the animals against people! You had cruel words whispered to them! What for, greedy king? What did you want to possess?" She took a deep breath and howled, "ENANTIODROMIA!"

She tugged her staff, and it was as if she had pulled out the king's soul and turned it inside out. For a moment the ice disappeared, and everything became black. Dimon was surrounded by people from both past and future. Spirits, faces, and events appeared to him as in a mirage, or fragments from a rainbow. Sunbeam came walking toward him, brightly clothed and transparent, looking as if her body was made of the aurora borealis. Dimon opened his arms and said, "Have you come back? I have missed you." The queen stopped and cast a sad eye over the battlefields he had left behind him, the blazing fires, the burned forests and devastated cities. Suddenly he saw himself, old and decrepit, in the middle of a ruined castle. He saw Obsidiana aging at a terrifying rate, his little treasure becoming old and gray, turning into a skeleton, and finally into dust that spiraled up and disappeared into the blackness. A whirlwind sucked up everything he had accomplished, until there was nothing left, not even a blade of grass. He heard someone hiss:

All vanishes
All dies
All is vain

The words echoed in his breast as if in an empty gold vault. The old woman twisted her staff, and it felt as though a knife were being twisted in a wound. Dimon opened his eyes and saw that he was standing on an ice sheet at the end of the world. He couldn't remember why he was there, but he felt cold. His teeth chattered. He looked around and asked, "Where is my child?"

The old woman released her grip and cried, "You think you have conquered the world, but I say this to you: No one conquers the world who cannot conquer time!"

The soldiers stood there as if frozen. "Do something!" Dimon shouted. "DO SOMETHING!" He brandished his sword, but the old woman cried, "All your wars are useless! TIME will destroy you in the end!"

She threw off her polar bear skin. She had the snout of a dog, seal-like fur, and webbed fingers. She cracked the ice with her staff, forming a hole through which she vanished into the deep blue waters of the ocean.

King Dimon headed home, silent. The faces of the frozen soldiers lined their route back. Ravens perched on the heads of those who had not already been gnawed through to the bone.

The War Against Time

The people of Pangea welcomed Dimon with brass bands and parades. The cobbled streets and the golden palace towers filled his heart with pride, but most of all he was looking forward to seeing Obsidiana. When he saw her there in her best blue dress, he hardly recognized her, she had grown so. She wished she could leap into his arms but, observing palace protocol, she extended her hand and recited the formal greeting she had learned:

"Welcome home, my father and king."

The king was dignified, as befits a king, and said: "Thank you; I am pleased to meet you, my dear daughter."

Obsidiana looked at her father. He didn't resemble the paintings, and his voice was different from what she had imagined. But there was no time to talk—a fanfare announced that they should go straight through to the banqueting hall, where they took their seats at each end of a long table, at which two hundred noble guests sat side by side celebrating with toasts and songs. Obsidiana had not seen these people before; all kinds of high commissioners and generals got to their feet to give long speeches. From now on the whole world would be ruled from the royal palace in Pangea.

Obsidiana could just barely glimpse her father at the far end of the table, until the main course created a mountain range between them—it was whole grilled elephant stuffed with a buffalo stuffed with a zebra stuffed with an antelope stuffed with a goat stuffed with a rabbit stuffed with a mouse that had a marinated crowberry stuffed up its rear end.

. Later, when the party guests had left and Obsidiana was ready for bed, the king came and sat with her. "It's good to be back again," he said, gently stroking her head.

"Thank you for all your letters," she said shyly. "But I much prefer having you here with me."

Through a ceiling window they could see stars twinkling. The king pointed at a red star that shone brighter than all the rest.

"I named that star after your mother; its name is Sunbeam. It watches over you and looks after you."

Obsidiana gazed at the star, enthralled, and felt a lump in her throat. The king took a letter from his pocket and handed it to her. It was written on calfskin and sealed with a golden signet.

"If anything happens, Obsidiana—if something should happen to me and you find yourself in trouble—you must open this letter. It will tell you the way to a cottage by a little lake, where your mother rests. You will be safe there. But you may only open this if all other options fail you."

Obsidiana observed his serious expression. She nodded and took the letter.

The king lightly kissed the top of her head. "You really are as graceful as a swallow," he said; he stroked her cheek and bade her good night. She felt how large and tender his hand was, how deep and resonant his voice. She smiled to herself. All was well now.

"Good night," she said, and fell into a deep and blissful sleep.

When she woke, something strange was going on. Though day had broken, it was not completely light, and from outside came the deafening noise of cawing and croaking.

Obsidiana looked out; the tops of the palace towers looked like black feathered hats—every surface was covered with mail crows. Birds soared around the turrets in the updraft, cawing so loudly you couldn't hear yourself think. She watched as courtiers armed with nets caught the birds, sorted the letters they brought, and put them into piles to take to the king. Obsidiana sat down to eat her breakfast; the king was nowhere to be seen.

"I guess he must be busy ruling the world," Thordis said. A day went past, a week, then another week, without her seeing her father. He was always in his office, ruling.

In the end, Obsidiana decided to go look for him. Clutching her panda, she slipped past people rushing hither and thither with all kinds of papers, and finally reached the king's office, where she found him sitting behind a gigantic pile of documents and regulations. An enormous map of the world hung on the wall behind him, and next to him stood Exel rattling off items from a long list:

"11,493 people have requested interviews, Sire, and 398 commissioners would like you to go on official visits. There are 3,578 laws for you to sign, 2,567 orders, 465 death warrants, and four reprieves. And there are still 14,522 crows waiting with unread messages."

"Let them wait," the king groaned, "I have to take a nap."

"I'm sorry, Sire, they'll eat the harvest if they wait too long. We released two thousand crows last night, but tomorrow we're expecting three thousand more with urgent petitions. The world won't rule itself."

Obsidiana shyly approached. The king looked up, gave her a weary smile and said: "Go into the yard and play a while. I'll be along shortly, there's an important letter I need to reply to."

Leading the panda, Obsidiana went gloomily out into the palace gardens, where she came across Jako. She sat down by the pond and watched the big goldfish swimming by. The little rhinoceros chewed on a piece of straw, and the deer were asleep beneath a toadstool.

"Silence soothes no sorrow," said Jako.

"Why is he so busy?"

"He who gathers all the sticks may be burned by the fire."

"But when will he be done with ruling the world?" Obsidiana said. "He has no spare time!"

"Probably never," said Jako. "The world is too big for one head."

The king was at the center of a web of power that encompassed the world, his head spinning over all the things that needed to be managed and controlled. He was always in meetings long before Obsidiana woke up, so could never say good morning, and usually didn't manage to say good night either. He wasn't sure whether he was a spider or a fly caught in its web.

"Do I have time to take Obsidiana to the little lake this summer?" he asked Exel.

"I'm afraid you're booked up three years and five months ahead."

"Isn't it sometimes better to rule more by ruling less?" the king asked, with hope in his voice.

"If a state is not ruled, it will fall apart," Exel said. When the king could finally go to bed, he looked in on Obsidiana. She was sleeping peacefully. She had grown so much that her toes peeked out from beneath her blanket. He went to his room, stretched himself out, and lay there unable to sleep. The moment he closed his eyes, the words of the woman on the ice rang in his head: *No one conquers the world who cannot conquer time.* All those years, all those victories meant nothing as long as time remained ungoverned. It was as if the words had been etched on his soul with the narwhal's tusk. *Time will destroy you in the end.* The moment when she touched him with her staff was fixed in his memory, and the chill would not leave his chest. Like a tune that sticks fast in one's brain, the words *All vanishes, All dies, All is vain* echoed around his hollow breast. He felt as if the crows were squawking:

"CRRROW CRAAGH AALL VANISHES! CRRROW CRAAGH AALL DIES! CRRROW CRAAGH AALL IS VAIN!"

A constant ticking in his head was driving him crazy. Tick, tick, tick, like an alarm clock or a tap dripping. Wherever he looked, it was the same; he felt as if the whole world was taunting him. The mountains towered over him, millions of years old. The waves laughed at him and crashed, as they would go on crashing forever. The stars twinkled and paid him no attention. He was nothing but a tiny bit of fluff that would soon blow away.

Wearily, the king trudged back to his office. He contemplated the pile of documents and the paintings of him and his beautiful princess. He looked at all the finery, the weapons and the vestments. What was it all for if in the end it would return to dust? If everything was to be swallowed up by time? He looked at the map that showed how his empire now stretched to the far edges of the world. He thought about all the places, all the wonders, all the food and luxuries, all the palaces he possessed but would never set foot in.

"How many palaces do I have?" he asked Exel.

"9,822," Exel replied.

"How long would it take to sleep one night in all of them?"

"246 years, including travel," Exel said.

"How much wine do I have?"

"197,185 gallons of fine wines."

"How long would it take me to drink it?"

"409 years if you drink five bottles a day."

"Could I rule my kingdom if I drank five bottles a day?"

"You wouldn't be able to walk, Sire," said Exel.

"How many stallions do I have?"

"54,983." He would never live long enough to ride all of them, either.

Dimon was enraged, and bellowed, "IT IS I who rule the kingdom! I reprieve men and sentence them to death, I win wars, I can depose gods and make people worship me instead, and yet I've been granted the same meager portion of time as the most miserable slave! A beggar might live to a hundred years while I could breathe my last tomorrow. Why conquer the world if the world then robs me of my time? Exel, you can change air into gold, you must know how to counter the cruelty of time."

Exel tapped something into his machine, shook his head, and said impassively:

"Unfortunately, this is the stark fact, Sire. You will grow old and die and ultimately be forgotten. Like everything else in the world, alas."

From his tower, the king watched Obsidiana running after the deer, Peak and Moon. The worst thing of all was that the greatest treasure in the world would grow old, decay, die, and be forgotten; she would vanish into the greedy maw of time just like her mother and all the other people that graced the paintings in his palace. He had left home for but a short while to conquer the world, but when he returned twelve years had passed.

Suddenly, it was as if Dimon came to his senses. He summoned all the kingdom's most senior officials and, gesturing to emphasize his words, he barked out the following order:

"Whosoever can find a way to preserve the youth and beauty of the princess, and enable me to conquer time, my most evil enemy, shall be rewarded with half my kingdom!"

Consiglio grew pale and the bees formed an exclamation mark above his head. He asked, as a counselor would be expected to do, "Is it really necessary to give away half of the kingdom?" Consiglio disguised the fact that his common sense was screaming, "HEAVENS PRESERVE US! THE KING HAS GONE TOTALLY CRAZY!"

But the king retorted, "What is half a kingdom worth to me if I have no time to enjoy it?" He pointed at a woman scrubbing the floor nearby. "Yes, if I am to live no longer than a menial scrubber!"

But the king didn't know that she was a wise, all-knowing woman. She shook her head and wrote with her cloth on the floor: *Be careful what you wish for!*

The king froze in his tracks. He stiffened and thundered, "What did you say?"

The woman looked up but ignored his question. Her eyes were completely white, like ostrich eggs.

"You do not control your fate—I do! To the lions!"

The king swept regally on his way while Consiglio stood by, ill at ease. To him it seemed as if the king was talking to himself—he saw no woman.

Feeding the Lions

The king's men went from town to town and from city to city, searching for somebody who could preserve time. They hunted for stories about elders and hermits who were supposed to have lived for hundreds of years. Outside the palace a multitude began to assemble; it was a colorful crowd, and King Dimon was greatly encouraged to see so many people waiting in a never-ending line to enter the royal audience chamber.

"I know a rhyme that will secure eternal life for the princess," a warlock said.

"I'm not sure that I believe you," said the king. "Who taught it to you?"

"My father."

"How old is he?"

"He died a long time ago," said the warlock.

"So, he didn't live forever, then!" said the king and waved him away.

A young man came in dragging a massive statue behind him. "This image of your daughter will perpetuate her name and her beauty forever, sire," he said.

"It is a beautiful work," said the king, "but what is the name on the plinth?"

"My name—Michael Hoggmin," said the artist, somewhat pleased with himself.

"And will somebody admire the beauty of this sculpture in a thousand years' time?"

"Yes," said the young man, with excitement. "People will admire it two thousand and three thousand years from now."

"And what will people read on the plinth: Michael Hoggmin? Did you intend to exploit the princess's beauty to secure eternal life for yourself?"

The sculptor trembled from head to toe as the king yelled, "Away with him! Feed him to the lions!"

And thus, the statue of the princess turned out to be Hoggmin's final masterpiece.

Over the days and weeks that followed, charlatans, artists, and poets flocked to the palace.

"Laughter lengthens life!" cried a clown, executing a pratfall.

"You overwhelm me with boredom," growled the king. "To the lions!"

Some old women appeared with ointments and lotions in clay pots, saying, "This elixir will guarantee eternal youth."

But the king asked brusquely, "Is this supposed to preserve my daughter's beauty? Then tell me, what has happened to your youth?"

Magicians and healers came, but the king shooed them all away. "Charlatans!" he yelled. "How dare you?"

And the king specifically forbade all kinds of ointments. He suspected his enemies of wanting to poison his daughter.

"I can fix her nose and stretch her skin as she gets older," said the plastic surgeon, opening his shiny box of knives; the king looked at them in horror.

"To the lions!" he ordered.

"I can make her immortal in verse," said the poet.

"'Face of porcelain'?" said the king when the poet had finished

47

reciting his poem. "Are you saying that her face is like a cup and saucer? Throw him to the lions!"

"I'm afraid that the lions are completely full, your Majesty," said Consiglio. "They couldn't even manage the plastic surgeon."

"To the crocodiles, then, or the poisonous bugs!" said the king.

"But I don't want to die!" cried the poet.

"Oh yes?" said the king caustically. "Didn't you say that your works made you immortal? Must I endure a fate that you refuse to suffer? Take him away!"

The poet was thrown screaming into a pit filled with poisonous bugs. The king went over to a window that overlooked the palace gardens; in the distance he could see Obsidiana, seated and stroking her white deer. She became more beautiful every day. She was opening like a rose. But to what purpose? Yes, what was the point of roses at all? Only to fade and remind us of the transience of the world.

Every day, people appeared before the king, but none brought the solution; the lions had lost their appetite, the poisonous bugs lay belly-up, and the boa constrictors burst like overcooked hot dogs. King Dimon was on the point of giving up. He rested his head in his hands and groaned, "Tomorrow is yet another day, and then it's evening again."

But suddenly important news arrived: A rumor was flying around the kingdom that a solution had been found and that it was, even now, making its way to the palace.

The Golden Centipede

A party of dwarfs was journeying toward the palace. They traveled on foot, drawing behind them a small carriage that bore a chest covered with a golden cloth. Everywhere they went they were the object of curiosity, and crowds gathered to watch and laugh at the procession as it passed by.

"He'll throw you to the lions!" they jeered. The dwarfs progressed at a snail's pace, step by step. Despite children throwing pebbles and orange peels at them, they pressed on undaunted. The tax collectors issued a bulletin reporting that the dwarfs had refused to allow any inspection of the chest's contents.

"Only the king may see what is inside the chest," said the leading dwarf.

"Otherwise we will return home," the next one said.

"And the king will not have the solution to his problem," said the third.

King Dimon ordered that they should be protected at all cost, and guards should escort them through bandit-ridden mountain passes. Farmers should feed them and merchants supply them with whatever they needed.

At long last they arrived at the city gates, footsore and covered with dust. With great ceremony they shouldered the chest and carried it up the main avenue, looking to all the world like a golden centipede. People gave way as they passed, and thus they proceeded along marble-paved streets up to the gilded palace.

Small and rustic, dirty and weary after their journey, the dwarfs went before the king and set the chest down in the center of the ceremonial hall, facing the throne. Courtiers followed them in, curious because dwarfs had never before been admitted to the palace—Dimon's forefathers had conquered their land, which was rich in hardwood, iron, copper, diamonds, and gold. The king tried to conceal his excitement by challenging their every statement.

"I starved the lions especially for you," he said. The courtiers laughed with their king. The leading dwarf stepped forward, doffed his yellow hat, and bowed.

"We are pleased to hear that, Your Majesty." The dwarf's shoes were badly worn, and his toes poked out.

The dwarf next to him finished the sentence, "But the lions will have to starve a little longer."

And the third said, "We bring you what you seek."

The fourth said, "We bring you three gifts."

The king eyed the leading dwarf with mistrust. If this was another charlatan, he would be severely punished. The dwarf bore a scar extending from forehead to chin, and one eyelid was cleft in two, exposing an all-white eye. A yellowed canine tooth could be seen through the split in his lip.

"What happened to you?" said the king.

"I would rather not talk about it."

"You may not conceal anything from me," said the king. "What happened?"

"Invaders raided my country, Sire, and killed nearly all of my family. A soldier slashed me with a knife as I lay in my crib, but I survived."

"What invaders?"

"It happened in your father's time, Sire, when he overthrew our state."

The king's face turned scarlet. "Insolent dwarfs," he whispered to Consiglio; his knuckles whitened as he gripped the handle of his sword. "You!" he thundered. "How dare you blacken my father's memory!"

The dwarf bowed humbly, gazing resolutely into the king's eyes. "You instructed me to tell you the truth. Should I have lied to you, Sire?"

"What is your business here?"

The dwarf took a deep bow. "The first gift we bring is an Albino Flower. It blooms once each century but only for a moment, then it withers."

The dwarfs went over to the chest and drew the golden cloth partly aside. The king peered through the crystal-clear glass of the lid at a flower that he had heard of only in fairy tales. An Albino Flower is rarer than a unicorn, according to myth. And yet here it was with its pale white stem and white foliage, this legendary flower that most people thought didn't actually exist. Delicate and complex, the flower was as semitransparent as a mirage.

"What kind of trick is this, dwarf? How can you preserve this flower?"

"I'm not here to perform magic tricks," said the dwarf, "I'm bringing you the truth." With that, he pulled the cloth off to reveal the remainder of the chest.

The king walked around it, stroking it with the palm of his hand.

At the other end of the chest lay a Falcon of Paradise. Seen at close quarters it was much more impressive than all the rumors about this mythical animal suggested. Its beak shone as if covered with silver; it had yellow and blue feathers, a mighty breast, and golden talons.

"Falcons of Paradise have accompanied the kings in your family for a thousand years, all of them except you," the dwarf

51

intoned, with what Dimon suspected was a hint of sarcasm. All the paintings and statues of Dimon's forefathers included images of Falcons of Paradise—but not Dimon's portrait.

"Falcons of Paradise became extinct fifty years ago," said the dwarf. "This is the last one."

"All that's missing now is a unicorn!" piped the court jester, and the hall exploded into laughter.

The dwarf waited patiently while the merriment subsided. "Now, pay attention. The casket is not made of glass. It is made of spider silk that is so tightly woven that time itself cannot pass through. When the casket is closed, time stops."

Red blotches appeared on the king's neck. "Really?" he said in disbelief. "So that falcon is neither stuffed nor asleep?"

"No," said the dwarf, "sleep is time. There is no sleep in the casket, no thought and no time. The Falcon of Paradise has no idea that fifty years have passed since it was placed in there. It seems frozen or asleep, but in fact, it is neither. Time cannot reach it. The falcon doesn't grow older, doesn't grow bigger, doesn't get gray, doesn't think, dream, or get hungry. It is timeless. The bird may appear stuffed, but the reality is that we have simply stopped time. As soon as we open the casket the flower will wither, and the falcon will fly out."

The king held his breath. Curiosity was almost killing him. "Open it and prove it!" The dwarf was in no hurry to obey. "Take a good look at the Albino Flower," he said. "This will be the only time you will ever see such a flower. You should allow more people to enjoy this moment. As soon as I open the casket, time will reach the flower and it will shrivel within seconds."

"Open the casket!" the king said testily.

"Very well," the dwarf said, sounding disappointed. Taking a long, last look at the flower, he placed his hands on the casket's lid. There was a sucking sound as a narrow slit let time in. The lovely Albino Flower turned black and dissolved like a piece of paper consumed by fire, turning into ashes. All that remained of it was some small threads that wafted away into the air. Everybody shouted in surprise, and then fell to the floor in alarm as the Falcon of Paradise took wing, shrieking and flying around the hall.

The king could hardly believe his own eyes. He applauded cautiously, not wanting to make a fool of himself.

"That was an interesting magic trick . . ." he said, ". . . an excellent magic trick. Thank you."

Another dwarf now stepped forward and threw a white dove into the air. The falcon gave chase, seized the dove with its talons, and flew to the king's throne, where it perched, pecking at its prey until there were feathers everywhere and its beak was stained red with blood.

The king feasted his eyes on the falcon. "Where did you get that bird? For twenty years my father sent people to seek out such a creature for me! A falcon like that is worth more than this palace!"

"It is the last of its kind, Sire. When this one dies the species will be officially extinct."

"Are you sure?"

"We know the forest. We kept this one, hoping to find a female to save the species. But the trees were all cut down."

"What for?" asked the king. The dwarf looked round, went over to one of the columns and tapped at it.

"Patagony wood," he said. "You all have expensive tastes."

The king felt his cheeks get hot. "Are you trying to provoke me?"

"No, Sire, I merely state facts." Dimon approached the casket again and knocked gently on it.

The dwarf continued. "As I have said, time cannot penetrate the spider silk. The falcon and the flower spent fifty years inside the casket. The bird was five years old when it was caught and is still five years old. The flower blooms for precisely one moment, and the casket preserved it in full bloom for fifty years. This casket has been the most sacred object in our family of dwarfs for many centuries."

"And of what use is such a casket to me?" said the king.

Hitherto silent, another dwarf now spoke up with passion. "A rose can rest in the casket for a thousand years without fading. An egg can remain there for centuries without going bad. A person could lie there for a hundred years, a thousand years, ten thousand years, completely protected from time. If you want to preserve your daughter's youth and beauty, she can lie in the casket for half a century without becoming a day older."

"Do you think I'm out of my mind? To shut my daughter away for half a century!"

The dwarf stepped back. "You asked for a solution, Your Majesty, and we have furnished it. It is up to you how, or whether, you use it. We have brought you protection against time and a key to eternal life."

The king looked searchingly at the dwarfs, these little men with their worn-out sheepskin shoes and expressionless faces.

"Is the casket a trap?"

"No, Your Majesty, dwarfs do not lay traps." The king didn't trust them, but he believed the evidence of his eyes. Meanwhile the falcon squawked shrilly: KWEEE! KWEEE!

The Magic Casket

The casket turned out to be the most wondrous object. The king gathered all the very best experts in the kingdom to investigate it. Goldsmiths, carpenters, denturists, blacksmiths, handymen, weavers, and diamond polishers scrutinized it and pored over it. They put an hourglass into it, and the sand stopped flowing as soon as the lid slammed shut. They filled it with butterflies that became suspended in midair like a mobile. Everybody agreed that this was the world's greatest masterpiece.

Exel knocked gently on the lid. "Just think how one might utilize such an object!" He took out his slide rule. "Last year there were one hundred sunny days and one hundred fifty rainy days. With a thing like this the princess could have been spared all that bad weather. Look at it today, windy and wet. What a waste of time! The princess should not spend her time in any conditions less than perfect, do you not think so, Sire?"

"Correct observation," said the king.

"If we add together all the rainy days and the merely overcast days, she had more than two hundred fifty completely wasted days last year. Imagine if you could choose just the good days and let the others go." He did some more calculating. "Your Majesty, if you only open the casket on Sundays she would be able to live for seven hundred years!"

The king gasped: seven hundred years!

"And if every other Sunday is rainy, she could live for fourteen hundred years. Then every day would be a sunny Sunday!"

"But what if the casket were only opened at Christmas?" asked Consiglio (who sometimes wished that every day was Christmas).

Exel calculated and was astonished by the outcome. "This cannot be right," he muttered and redid the calculation. "Thirty-six thousand five hundred years!"

Consiglio reddened. "Sire, you promised half your realm to anybody who could give you more time. It seems to me that the dwarfs have fulfilled that requirement. What are you going to do? You can't hand half your kingdom over to the dwarfs, can you?"

Exel was quick with an answer. "According to my calculations it's better to own half a kingdom for thirty-six thousand years than a whole kingdom for a hundred years. But first we must test the casket on the princess."

Summoned by the king, Thordis brought Obsidiana into the hall.

"Look, my daughter!" he said merrily. "Some dwarfs have come with a gift for you!"

The dwarfs were presented, wearing the new clothes that the king had had made for them. She waved, and one of the dwarfs bowed to her, making her blush.

"They've brought us a magic casket that will give us more time," said the king. "I would like you to try it out."

"A magic casket?" she said. She peered through its transparent walls at the pillow and white silken coverlet inside.

She looked around at all the courtiers waiting in suspense, and at the impassive faces of the dwarfs. She climbed into the casket and laid her head on the pillow. "Now count to ten!" said the king.

Obsidiana closed her eyes and started to count. "One, two, three, four . . . " THUMP! The casket closed and then opened again.

" . . . five, six, seven . . . " Obsidiana opened her eyes. The king was standing over her and Exel was recording in his notebook every detail of what happened. "Aren't you going to close it?" she asked.

"The casket was closed for ten minutes," said the king.

They closed it again, and once more Obsidiana said: "Aren't you going to close the casket?"

"It was closed for an hour," said the king, laughing. They closed the casket yet again.

Obsidiana looked around and screwed up her eyes. The sun was blazing, and yet only a moment ago it had been windy and raining. She jumped to her feet. In what seemed a fraction of a second, Thordis had changed into a different dress and put up her hair. How could she switch clothes so quickly? Obsidiana ran to the big doors that led to the palace gardens and pushed them open. The cherry trees were heavy with blossom. She gasped—it was so beautiful. She had been looking forward to the spring so much. And now it was here.

"How did the trees come into leaf so quickly?"

"It happened very slowly; it took ten days. You simply didn't notice."

"We closed the casket on April fifth. Now it's April fifteenth." Exel stood there, excited, with his slide rule. "You have saved ten days!"

Obsidiana was puzzled. This could not be true. There was a different scent in the air—the scent of spring and warmth, a heavy smell of earth. She ran off, looking for her panda.

"Panda!" she cried. But the red animal stuck its tail in the air and hissed as she drew near.

"The panda lay on the casket whining the whole time," said Thordis. "It thought you were dead. You can't explain these things to animals."

Obsidiana ran to her room and leafed through her diary. She paged through the empty days. This was baffling. She had no memory of these days, they had simply disappeared. She wrote:

Dear diary, there are some days missing here. Some dwarfs came with a magic casket. I lay down in the casket and ten days disappeared in a flash. Where did the time I lost go? Can I get it back?

High up in the glass tower, the king was sitting at an enormous round table. On the wall he had projected an outline of the kingdom he had spent the last decade fighting for. In his hand was the declaration:

Whosoever can bring me or my daughter more time shall be rewarded with half my kingdom.

It was clear that the dwarfs had fulfilled the requirement: This was truly a magic casket, and with it he would be able to protect his daughter from the ravages of time. The dwarfs were entitled to half the kingdom.

Kingdom of the Dwarfs

Palace guards escorted the dwarfs to attend the king. Dimon decided to tread carefully; small they might be, but they could be capable of anything. One who has the patience to weave thread for such a magic casket also has the patience to wreak vengeance.

"Why did you weave the casket?" he asked.

"Life in the mountains can be harsh; we used it to store food," said one dwarf.

"But then we put the falcon in the casket," added another.

"What about people?"

"No, it was never used for people."

"Why not?"

"It just didn't occur to us, I suppose," said the dwarf.

"Why did you bring the casket to me? Is it dangerous?"

"No," said the dwarf, "the casket itself is not dangerous. The danger lies with whoever possesses it. You need maturity and wisdom to manage such a thing." His expression seemed inscrutable, enigmatic.

"Is this a trap, some kind of instrument of vengeance?" said the king.

"We were completely vanquished by your army," said the dwarf. "Most of the precious metals have been dug out of our mountains. Your father and your grandfather fought us with fire, but revenge is not part of our culture. The casket is now in your hands. It is up to you whether it will be for your good or ill."

The king regarded the dwarf for a long time. "The casket is small, it might fit my daughter, but it won't fit me. Can you make another one for me?"

"In return for the other half of the kingdom?" the dwarf chuckled.

"For a reasonable sum," the king said.

"No," was the curt response.

"NO? What do you mean NO? I refuse to accept such an answer!"

"Such a casket can never be made again. My grandmother and my mother knew how to weave the fabric for the casket. They stroked the spiders to spin their thread, and it took forty years to weave it."

"Call them here!"

The dwarf drew a finger across his face. "I was slashed with a knife as I lay in my crib and yet I survived. Though my grandmother fled, my mother, sisters, and cousins were not so lucky."

"That had nothing to do with me."

The dwarf stepped closer to the king. The guards stiffened. Up in the rafters an archer drew his bow, taking aim at the dwarf's heart. "The head of an octopus does not always know what the tentacles are doing, Your Majesty."

King Dimon looked long and hard at the dwarf and at the onlookers. Finally he said, loud enough for all to hear, "Enough is enough, dwarf. You have delivered the solution to my quest." Casting his gaze over the assembled company, he proclaimed: "The king's promise stands. I gave my oath that whoever could stop time and preserve my daughter's beauty would gain half my kingdom. Here it is, dwarfs! It is your lawful possession!"

And, striding over to the map that hung on the wall, he drew his knife and cut it in two.

The hall fell silent. The generals turned scarlet. Was he really, after all these wars, going to give half his kingdom to a bunch of dwarfs?

Dimon turned back to the dwarf with the split eye. "Are you prepared to assume power over half my realm? Will the people swear allegiance to you, dwarf king?"

The dwarf looked at the king, his expression still inscrutable. "There is nothing, O King, that you can give us. Nothing can compensate for what you have taken from us. The bird, the flower, and the casket were all that we had left. Now you have a time casket for your daughter. You have eternity in your hands. Use it wisely, but half a kingdom is of no use to us. We decline your offer."

There was rustling in the hall. The king's face reddened. "My words stand," he said. "Half the kingdom is yours; that was the agreement."

"We want nothing. You do not keep your promises; you deserve everything that the future holds for you." The dwarf gazed directly into the king's eyes.

"What do you mean: everything that the future holds for me? Is that a curse?"

"I said merely that you deserve all that the future holds for you, whether good or bad. That is how it is."

The dwarfs prepared to leave. Those present fell silent. "This is an insult!" the king thundered. "You mock me! I promise you half the kingdom, and you refuse it! You give me a casket, a magic flower, and a Falcon of Paradise, but you won't accept anything in return!" The king bit his lip and shook with anger. "My only option is to sentence you to death. If you ask for mercy, then at least I will have granted you your lives. If not, then the casket is the spoils of war. I shall never treat it as a gift."

The dwarfs looked at him. Some seemed about to faint, but the one with the scar said: "Good. That is perfect. We would not wish to owe our lives to your grace and mercy."

The guards seized the dwarfs, shackled them, and transported them to the city stadium, where they were caged alongside hulking berserkers, lions, and tigers.

Three times Dimon's messenger came to them, saying, "The king offers you pardon; how do you respond?"

The dwarfs spat at the messenger. Eventually the king himself came in the shadow of night, lit by the glow of a flaming torch.

"Will you accept my mercy?" But the dwarfs stared at him from the darkness of their prison and said nothing.

At dawn a burly executioner came to see them. Bare to the waist, he was hairy as an ape and covered with scars. He wore a top hat. Vicious combat and lingering deaths were his specialty. He sized the dwarfs up and roughly jammed ridiculous helmets onto their heads.

"The funniest thing in the world is dwarfs being chased by lions!" he bellowed.

Guards gave the dwarfs swords and shields that were too big, and propelled them into the arena. They were met by a roar of cheering and boisterous laughter. But when the gratings were raised and ravenous lions came charging into the stadium, the dwarfs lay down flat on the stone floor of the arena. The beasts sniffed around them but left them untouched. The angry crowd went wild and bayed for blood. In the royal box, the king sat and watched the display in silence; there was a lead weight in the pit of his stomach, and the gold vault in his breast had never felt so empty. He sweated and felt as if he was choking in the heat. The lion-keeper, cursing and scarlet with embarrassment, entered the arena and shooed the lions back into their cages. Gladiators now took the stage, but the dwarfs refused to fight—even after being thrashed with whips and jabbed with spears.

"Goddamned useless combat, this!" the executioner muttered.

The mob booed and threw tins and clay pots into the arena. "BLOOD! BLOOD! BLOOD!"

An entertaining battle between dwarfs and lions was obviously not going to happen; there was no way to get them to fight. The executioner, in a black hood and armed with a mighty ax, entered the arena. The dwarfs lay motionless, even when he prodded them with the handle of his ax, so he set about his task and chopped the head off the first dwarf where he lay stock-still on the ground. The mob booed.

He moved to the next one, and thus he axed the dwarfs one after another. They offered no resistance, but the dwarf with the scar fixed his gaze on the king, sitting there in the royal box. The executioner raised his ax high up in the air and brought it down with all his strength. To the king it felt as if the impact of it lasted all day long. For a long time afterward he was able to replay in his mind every single moment from when the executioner raised his ax until it cracked down on the ground. He could recall the pattern on the executioner's tunic and the grin on the dwarf's face that turned sad in the moment before his head flew off. When the ax struck the stone floor, he felt a rush of air and a heavy pounding beneath their feet like the forewarning of an earthquake. The crowd fell silent as the dwarf's head bounced onto the ground. Thunderstruck, the executioner looked down at his ax and saw that the stone floor had split beneath its blade. There was a creaking sound as the ground began to slide apart.

The stadium split into two, and a crack stretched like a fine seam all the way through the city. The crack became a rift, then a ravine, and then a canyon. It filled with water and became a channel, a bay, and finally a turbulent ocean. The crack split the city and the whole of the kingdom into two. Pangea became what we today know as the continents of South America and Africa.

A Dwarf's Head

Grace closed the book. The kids were silent. Night had fallen.
"Well, it's time to go to bed," she said.
"Did he really chop the dwarfs' heads off?" Peter asked.
"Yes, he did," Grace said.
"Why?"
"The king had to keep his word."
"Wasn't he a kind man?"
"Kind? He conquered the whole world. How can a man like that be kind?"
"I don't believe that a single ax can split the continents!"
"What do I know?" Grace said. "Look at nuclear weapons. A piece of radioactive metal the size of a fist can bomb a whole city to smithereens. At one time that might have been called magic metal. Maybe the dwarfs knew something we don't know. They could make the most amazing objects from gold and rocks, and they were able to weave a casket from spider's web silk. The story goes that in those days, while other humans had an accord with the animal kingdom, the dwarfs had an accord with the earth; they may well have been able to join continents or split them apart if they wanted to."

She reached up into a cupboard and brought out a broken vase.

"Look at this," she said. "This was a broken vase that I glued back together. Half of it was found in Africa and the other half in South America."

"But how come the continents split apart so quickly?"

"That was precisely what the Pangeans asked themselves."

Kristin was evidently exhausted by now and yawned loudly. Grace went and fetched blankets and pillows and bedded the children down. Sigrun tried to keep one eye open—you couldn't trust anybody—but when the kids fell asleep one by one, she finally nodded off too.

She woke to the appetizing smell of hot oatmeal. Rubbing the sleep from her eyes, she joined the other kids sitting at a long table, greedily devouring their breakfast. A deer out in the yard glanced up abruptly and bolted. Sigrun was starving and decided to try having just a little bite to eat.

Grace had loosened her braid, and her hair looked gray and unkempt.

"Right, who wants to help Marcus catch fish for lunch?" she said.

Sigrun was eager to get out of the house, and quickly offered to go. "Don't forget the bat," said Grace, handing Marcus a baseball bat.

Sigrun didn't like the look of this. "Are you going to catch fish with that?" she said.

"No, the bat is for the wolves," said Marcus.

"Or the zombies," said Grace.

Sigrun's face fell. *Zombies?*

"Only joking," Grace said and laughed. "But there are wild animals out there, so you must be careful."

Sigrun and Marcus headed off. Birds sang in the trees. The two stood to one side as a moose came trotting along the road and stopped to rub its butt against a fence post. "How do you know Grace?" Sigrun asked.

"I don't know her," Marcus said. "She found me like I found you. My dad had been finalizing the takeover of some big Finnish company and Mom was completing her PhD. I broke a window in school and was suspended for a week. That was when my folks brought one of those TimeBoxes® home; they said they didn't have time to cope with me, let alone look after me for a whole week."

"So what happened?"

"I climbed into the box; the next thing I knew, Grace was standing in front of me in her black dress. It was like a nightmare. I tried to run off, but I was alone in the world and everything was covered with briars and brambles, so I stopped. Grace stood waiting for me, but she scared me. She turned back home and then I heard the wolves on the hill, so I thought I had better follow her. She showed me all the old stuff she's collected and said she was trying to find out what went wrong with the world."

Sigrun looked back toward her neighborhood—or rather toward the forest where the neighborhood used to be.

"Can we stop by my house?" she asked.

"Why?"

"I need to release Mom and Dad from their caskets."

"You can't," Marcus said.

"Why not?"

"Grace says it's not possible."

Sigrun gazed at the houses that lined the lake. They were in a state of near collapse, as were the old jetties. A Ferris wheel floated half-submerged in the middle of the lake; it must have rolled there from a nearby carnival. The sun was up, and the surface of the water was mirror-smooth. A pair of swans swam in the distance, and somewhere there was a loon calling. They came across a nest on the bank occupied by a plump eider duck that didn't move even when they walked very close to it. Taking an orange rowboat, they paddled out toward a red plastic can

floating near the Ferris wheel. Marcus stowed the oars, grabbed
the can, and began to haul in the fishnet that was attached to
it. At first all they could see was white blurs in the depths of the
water, but he soon dragged the bulging net aboard, full of lovely,
plump trout that wriggled at their feet. Sigrun freed one from
the net and knocked it out on the gunwale.

In the center of the lake stood a rusty sign:

SKIP THE CRISIS! TimeBox®

Marcus pointed at the sign. "It's those people's fault. TimeBox®
has messed up the world. They're responsible for all this."

"But I don't see what we can do," Sigrun said.

"I don't know any more than you do," Marcus said. "But
maybe Grace does. I can't see that we have any choice other
than to listen to the story. I don't think we have anything to
lose, either."

They walked back home with armfuls of trout. The street was
like a ravine, with trees growing out through broken windows.
Seagulls had nested on windowsills and the edges of roofs; they
soared in the updraft, wailing mournfully. Sigrun looked up.

"It's beautiful," she said.

"Yes."

"My feet are wet; I wish I had some new rubber boots."

"If you go to the mall there won't be much left of you aside
from your boots," said Marcus.

"Oh?"

"I hear there were bears there yesterday when the kids went
to get some tinned food. They had found the honey jars. Better
to stay away."

*

Outside the house they found Grace peeling potatoes with Kristin. They gave her the trout, which she took into the kitchen, cut in pieces, and put in a pot to cook. Soon the children were enjoying a tasty meal. As they ate, Grace opened a glass cabinet and took out an ancient skull.

"Look at this, isn't it lovely?" she said. Sigrun almost choked on her food.

Grace pointed at a dent in the skull. "Someone struck this person in the face during childhood, but the wound has healed." Sigrun could see a mark stretching from one eye socket down to the jaw.

Grace turned the skull round and showed Sigrun a fracture of the occipital bone.

"Much later the whole head was chopped off."

"Is that the dwarf?" Sigrun asked.

"Everything I'm telling you is based on reliable sources," said Grace, handing Sigrun the skull. Sigrun shuddered and almost dropped it.

Kristin and Peter giggled. The kids made themselves comfortable, and Grace continued her story.

The City that Disappeared

In a glass-like casket next to King Dimon's empty throne lay the most beautiful maiden anybody had ever seen—her skin white as snow, her lips red as blood, her hair black as a raven's wing. She lay at rest in the casket, still as a porcelain doll, oblivious of the colossal events that assailed the kingdom.

CRRREEEAK! CRRREEEAK! The earth shuddered and shook. Dimon rode along the edge of the rift with his advisers. He watched as the two halves of Pangea moved away from one another like gigantic aircraft carriers. He watched the torn-apart stadium and the houses teeter on the edge before plunging into the void. You could hardly hear yourself speak above the subterranean rumbling as the gap widened and filled with the roar of crashing waves.

Exel stood petrified at the sight of the world's biggest line being drawn. "Are you sure this is a rift?" he asked.

"What do you mean?" Dimon said.

"According to my accounts this is impossible—it's completely impossible for this to happen! Completely impossible!"

Dimon approached the edge and dropped a stone; it fell and fell and fell. He saw crowds of people gathering on each side of the split. He saw lovers gazing at each other, full of longing, separated by a rift that only birds could cross. He saw suspension bridges turning into enormous slingshots as they stretched and then snapped, propelling unfortunate travelers miles into the distance. The lucky ones didn't do too badly if a bush or a mossy knoll softened their landing, but others ended up plastered onto walls or rocks like fat bees on a windshield, and those who landed in the water were devoured by hungry sharks.

Messengers came from all directions—sweaty and breathless, having ridden their horses to death.

"Your Majesty! Pangea has been completely split in two."

Scheming dwarfs! Dimon thought. *So they managed to divide my kingdom after all!*

"And we bring tragic news from the south: Obsidiana City has disappeared."

"Disappeared?" said the king. "Cities don't just disappear!"

"It's true, it's totally disappeared!"

"What about the people?"

"Not a trace, Sire. What can we do?"

Hurriedly, Dimon wrapped himself in a black cloak and rode off. He flew along the flagstoned path through the dark forest he knew so well, but where the city was supposed to greet him, bright and sparkling, he saw only a fathomless, wild sea. He looked through the gaping city gates and saw nothing but a void. Rocks tumbled from the gash in the earth and tree roots stuck out from the rock face like the hands of drowning men. His horse reared, neighing; poised precariously on the cliff's edge, Dimon rubbed his eyes in disbelief. There was supposed to be a castle here, a thriving city with smoke coiling from its chimneys—he should be hearing the street calls of peddlers, the laughter of children, and the chanting of monks. A foul stench rose from the water, and he tried not to think about what caused it. He grimaced and gritted his teeth. How could the land split apart so suddenly?

He recalled the prophetic words of the old hag in the north who had plunged into the hole in the ice shouting *Enantiodromia! Time will destroy you!* Was she in cahoots with the dwarfs? Time, accursed time!

On his way back to the palace he met Jako, the philosopher. He sat down by him and asked anxiously: "What can I do? How can I solve a problem that defeats a million minds?"

"I thought you wanted to rule the world. That's plenty of work in itself," said Jako, calmly puffing at his pipe. "Now you have enough on your plate."

"What kind of wisdom is that supposed to be?" asked the king.

"All I've ever wanted to do is to puff at this pipe," said Jako. "Then I'd have enough time to do nothing on my days off."

"I wish time would drown in camel dung!" Dimon thundered.

Songs of grief echoed around the kingdom.

> *I rode home to Golden City*
> *a wife and seven children*
> *waiting there*

> *I rode home to Golden City*
> *I found nothing*
> *nothing there*

> *I rode home to Golden City*
> *lost in the forest*
> *my heart was bare*

In the same manner that Obsidiana City went, Silk City disappeared, and the Golden City split into two. The burden of the whole world rested on Dimon's shoulders. *My heart has been threaded on a narwhal's tusk*, he thought.

All the world knew of the rift—everyone, that is, except the lovely Obsidiana, lying in the casket of time, an innocent smile on her lips. King Dimon was pleased; it was good that she didn't have to feel fear or lie awake while the earth trembled and the world was torn apart. Obsidiana escaped not just all the terror but also historic world events and omens of peril. As well as daily occurrences like morning dew, evening mist, sunsets and sunrises, she missed out on a solar eclipse and the spring when seventy rainbows were seen on the same day. She missed the day of the Great Heartbreak, when half of the kingdom officially disappeared over the horizon and the rift became an ocean. She was not present when the citizens of Pangea gathered together along the full length of the coastline on both sides of the rift. In tears, people waved silk flags as the last turrets and mountain peaks disappeared into the distance. Lovers and sweethearts, friends and relatives and dear neighbors were parted forever.

But Obsidiana lay still, innocent. She couldn't know that she would soon be idolized and adored, but that, later, people would come to fear her more than darkness itself.

Obsidiana Saved from Boredom

The whole of Pangea was in turmoil. In the chaos following the rift, grocers turned into looters, tax collectors into blackmailers, fishermen into pirates, and squads of soldiers into rioting mobs. Farmers abandoned their farms and became wandering beggars when their livestock was stolen and their crops were torched. King Dimon needed to draw on all his resources to halt a descent into anarchy, but there were evil rumors that he was losing his mind—that he had stood for a whole night in a palace corridor staring into a corner as if at a ghost. Consiglio came upon him standing there and asked:

"What are you looking at, your Majesty?"

"Shush! Don't you see?" Dimon whispered. "It's time—seize it!"

Sentries stood guard over the casket twenty-four hours a day. They stared dumbstruck at this innocent beauty; she must be holy, she must be from another world. The king had decreed it forbidden to frighten Obsidiana unnecessarily. Nobody might disturb her and allow the cruelty of time to afflict her.

The sun ran its customary course from east to west across the sky, ignorant of the misery and disasters that filled every day. They could only open the casket on a day that was perfect, but such a thing was a rare occurrence. Exel and his advisers met every morning to review the day and speculate on the likelihood of earthquakes in the morning or cloud cover in the evening.

"The sun is out," said one long-bearded expert, "but it's a little windy . . ."

"Yes, and maybe not quite warm enough," said another. "What about the horoscope?"

"Not particularly good," the first one said.

"So our conclusion? Is the day worthy of her?"

"No! Save it!"

"Save it!"

"A day retained is a day gained."

Sunny days had to be very special to be good enough for such a precious princess. Whenever the casket was opened, thick drapes were drawn across any windows that faced the Great Rift. Nobody was to mention rebellions, riots, dwarfs, or anything else that could cast a shadow over Obsidiana's happiness. Nobody was to talk about time, what happened in the past or what lay ahead, since she might become sad if she heard about fun occasions she had missed.

The world skipped past Obsidiana, and time became a strange thing to her. By royal decree, every single day of Obsidiana's life outside the casket was to be full of activities. Instead of wandering aimlessly around the palace as had been her wont, she followed a schedule that organized every last detail of her day.

After the darkness of winter a lovely summer had arrived and so the casket was opened. Obsidiana screwed up her eyes against the unaccustomed light of the sun. Breakfast was served to the accompaniment of jolly music, and she had scarcely swallowed her last mouthful when Consiglio appeared with seven butterflies fluttering around his head like a crown. Then a fanfare sounded and her father appeared with his falcon. She fed the falcon raw pigeon meat and was allowed to don leather gloves and carry it. Its claws were sharp as knives. Obsidiana noticed a black-clad man standing to one side holding a large hourglass and signaling to the king. Her father looked worried so she said:

"What's troubling you, Papa?"

"Oh, it's nothing, my little lamb. Everything is going well. Everything is flourishing. The world is perfect."

Running barefoot into the palace gardens Obsidiana encountered Thordis, who embraced her warmly. Obsidiana whispered: "What's happened? Why is everybody so strange?"

"Nothing," replied Thordis dryly. "Nothing's happened. Everything is flourishing. The world is perfect."

Obsidiana lay down in the casket, and the next time it opened a lovely spring day greeted her. She thought: *Wasn't it summer yesterday? How could it have been summer yesterday and spring today?* Thordis came and hugged her even more tightly and lovingly than usual, as if she had just arrived back from a long journey.

"How I've missed you, my child."

"But I saw you only yesterday!" Obsidiana said.

"No, my dear, I've waited a long, cold winter to see you."

Obsidiana was confused. Thordis had changed. It was as if the flowers that blossomed yesterday had fled back into the safety of their buds. She was perplexed: *Did I miss the birds migrating, the autumn leaves, and the winter snow?*

This day passed like the previous one except that it was even more tightly planned, so that Obsidiana fell asleep exhausted.

She slept all night but woke to the noise of a storm raging outside. The black-clad timekeeper rang a bell: Save time! Save time!

Ladies-in-waiting ran into the room and helped Obsidiana into the casket once more. The next day arrived a moment later.

By now it was summer, and a whole choir stood waiting to sing "Happy Birthday" to her.

"Birthday?" she said. "Haven't I just had a birthday?" But there was no time to think, as her father arrived bearing an enormous birthday cake and she forgot everything in her joy.

She felt almost seasick at the way everybody's appearance kept changing. People looked as if they were made of clay or some kind of putty that pulled and stretched. Everybody near her smiled. And yet, though no one said anything about it, people seemed worried; she noticed that they stared at her but avoided meeting her eye.

"Obsidiana is acting strangely; she looks at me like I've put on weight," whispered one of the maids as she was going to bed.

"She looks at me as if she's counting my wrinkles," said another.

Although the days were fun and there was plenty going on, Obsidiana missed the companionship of her panda. It cowered in a corner when she approached.

"Is something wrong, dear panda?" she said, but the panda arched its back and growled.

Obsidiana wandered over to the pond in the palace gardens, where old Jako was sitting on a bench. She sat down beside him, deep in thought, and said:

"It's my birthday today, but I've only just had a birthday. I don't know how old I am anymore. Do you know how old I am?"

But old Jako didn't hear what she said. She looked at him. She hardly recognized this gaunt, stooping figure with the wizened face, but he smiled his bright smile when he saw her. Obsidiana repeated her question, speaking louder. Jako closed his eyes and said in his wise voice: "Never keep anything! Give the bread when new and the flower before it fades. Happiness drinks what boredom brews."

Obsidiana wasn't happy with this answer and ran off to find her nurse.

"How old am I?"

"What do you mean?" said Thordis.

"I've had sixteen birthdays, but I haven't lived for sixteen years. Only a few days passed between my fourteenth and fifteenth birthdays, and there was no summer when I was thirteen. All the other days disappeared."

"I haven't counted the days, but you must be twelve or thirteen years old. You should ask Exel. He has it all logged." Obsidiana turned and was about to run off but then she heard Thordis curse under her breath.

"What's the matter, Nursie dear?" she asked.

"I hate this casket business," she said. "I think nothing good will come of it."

Gunnhild

The day came when the king took a new queen. Born to a noble family, Gunnhild was fair and wise, spoke eleven languages, could dance and sing and weave, and, most importantly, she always agreed with the king—Exel had her take a special test to be sure of that.

The marriage took place amid great pomp and ceremony and was celebrated throughout the kingdom with parades and music. Obsidiana smiled from ear to ear throughout the wedding feast.

"Look how happy she is," the king said.

"Yes," Gunnhild said hesitantly. "But aren't you going to open the casket?"

"No, it isn't the right time. See how happy she is now; it would be a shame to spoil that by surprising her."

An odd look came over Gunnhild's face. "You're probably right. Let's wait for the right moment."

Thordis was at the reception, looking like a thundercloud. She confronted Exel. "Obsidiana needs to have a life, too! She needs to grow up. First you say that no other child is worthy of her and now it's not the right time to introduce her to the new queen. Where are the friends she was promised?"

"It's not an easy thing to comprehend," said Exel dryly, "but if we'd allowed Obsidiana to have friends they would now be much older than she. They would long since have grown away from her."

Thordis grew pale. She hadn't thought of this. "That's terrible," she said. "Are you saying she will never know friendship?"

"Do you think a brief friendship is more important than eternity? Is a friend more important than life itself?"

"You all are out of your minds! I'm not allowed to tell her about the world anymore. How can I bring up a child whose worldview is an illusion? How will Obsidiana succeed to her father's throne if she has no idea of the ways of things?"

"She doesn't need to know anything," said Exel. "The king will have fixed everything before she ascends to the throne."

"The king isn't going to live forever!"

"But she will, if she doesn't waste her life unnecessarily," Exel said calmly.

Thordis shook her fist at him. "The dwarfs warned against this! They didn't use the casket for themselves! They said that you need wisdom to manage it."

"Are you saying the king lacks wisdom?" Exel was outraged. Thordis stormed out of the room, biting back her tears.

The next time the casket was opened, Gunnhild was away on a trip and nobody was allowed to tell Obsidiana about her. Obsidiana slipped away from a circus performance and snuck back to her room, where she sat leafing through her diaries. The royal bookbinder made her a new book every year, bound in green crocodile hide and with a golden spine. All her old diaries were packed with entries right up until the day the casket arrived, when her entry had been very brief:

Today was a lovely day; some dwarfs came to see us with a magic casket . . .

Then there were gaps, and more gaps, and then almost a whole year that was completely blank. After that there were two books in which she had only written about one spring day and her birthday. Had she lost all the other days? She took out the newest diary and wrote in the correct place:

The days are weird. Yesterday was summer and today is summer too, but it isn't the same summer! I had put a mark on one of my trees and it's grown by a whole foot, but everyone pretends that everything is normal! I feel as if everyone's a little lopsided. When Nursie cuddled me I saw a new wrinkle on her forehead. She had tears in her eyes and said she had missed me so much. But how can I miss her? I only saw her a moment ago! She's been waiting for me for a whole year, although she doesn't speak about it. I had a birthday "yesterday." Also a few days ago. I can't miss anybody, and I can't look forward to anything! I'm confused. What is "time," actually? What is it that changes a puppy into a big dog, that draws green sprouts from a seed and turns them into a huge tree in a moment? What treats old people so harshly that they crumble and die?

She leafed through the empty pages, and tears began to run down her cheeks. She felt she saw her father every day, but according to the diaries it was only a few occasions a year. Why was she not allowed to take part in his time? The tears flowed, and her sobbing was heard out in the corridor. There was much agitation in the palace. Was the immortal princess unhappy? What had gone wrong? They summoned the king.

"Don't cry, my dear daughter. I know this has been a strange time."

"Yes."

"But it will get better. You will inherit the world you deserve. But for that to happen we must go on a long journey all the way to the farthest limits of the kingdom in the west."

"Amazing!" said Obsidiana, wrapping her arms around his neck. "A long journey!"

The king shook his head and drew back a little so that Obsidiana let go of him.

"Not 'we' as in you and me," he said; "'we' as in me, the army, and the lawyers. It will be a hazardous journey. We have built ships that can sail across the rift. Nobody's done that before."

"What rift?"

"That's nothing for you to worry about," the king said. "It's just something that needs fixing."

Saddened, Obsidiana asked: "How long?"

"At least two years." Everything seemed to go black, and anger raged inside her head. She had waited long enough. She had been promised time, she had been promised she could visit the forest grove, travel, and see the world. All her life she had dreamed of having fun friends, of seeing burnished turrets, verdant fields, unicorns grazing, and covered bridges over lakes full of swans.

"But you promised!" she cried. "We were going to visit Obsidiana City when you returned."

"There is something of a problem there," said Dimon hesitantly.

"You promised that everything would be fine when you had conquered the world!"

"You know the casket. A whole year for me is but a moment for you. I'm the one who will miss you; you won't notice my absence. We'll close the casket and before you know it—I'll be back with you." The king kissed her forehead and said: "Just remember, we'll see each other again in a moment!"

So the ladies-in-waiting led Obsidiana to the casket, which glittered like a dew-spangled spider's web on a fall morning. Anxiously, Obsidiana absorbed the last moments of another day that would never return. Outside the sun shone, a swallow sat on a branch singing, a fly buzzed. She lay down in the casket and closed her eyes.

"Now smile," said her father. She gave a faint smile, which froze on her lips as the casket snapped shut. The king made Exel and Gunnhild solemnly swear not to let anybody disturb the princess's repose. Her sensitive heart must not be burdened with regret or worry.

Obsidiana lay within the casket in a frozen moment, like a fly in golden amber. Her skin was white as snow, her lips as red as blood, her hair as black as a raven's wing.

> *Graceful as a swallow,*
> *guileless as a lamb,*
> *golden is her beauty—the whole world's charm.*

A Goddess Is Born

Time hammered at the casket like a waterfall. It tried to squeeze itself through the tiniest chinks but not even a fraction of a second found a way through. Meanwhile the king sailed across the Great Rift, which by now had become an angry ocean. With his ten-thousand-strong army he passed beyond the tall mountains and rode across deserts into the heart of the war zone, leaving his palace in the hands of Exel and Queen Gunnhild.

During his absence the queen amused herself giving banquets for the nobility, who flocked to the palace. Her aristocratic guests gasped when Gunnhild showed them into the chamber where the casket stood like a gigantic crystal.

"How beautiful she is! She is just as she was four years ago. How is this possible?"

Wise men came from distant corners of the world to see this phenomenon.

"Where is the soul while she lies in the casket in this timeless state?" they asked.

"It must be with the gods," Gunnhild said. "It's the only possible answer."

The wise men were astonished. "With the gods?"

"Of course. How else could she be free of time? I put a gold necklace on the lid of the casket and asked her to take my prayer to the gods. The wish came true and I discovered the healing powers of the casket."

"Really?"

"Yes, my tennis elbow was cured when I touched the lid."

"May I try?" one of the wise men asked.

"You can try," said Gunnhild, "but the princess will only cure those who please her. You will have to offer a piece of jewelry or some object that you prize to prove that you really mean what you say."

Tales of miracles ran like wildfire around the kingdom. A young man put a gold ring on the casket lid and asked Obsidiana to take a message to the goddess of love. He won the girl he desired. Another brought silver coins and asked for rain. He got what he wanted. A woman asked the fertility goddess for a baby and had twins. There was clearly a need for miracles among the citizens of Pangea—the aristocracy lined up to visit the palace, and soon the common people wanted to come too. The rift dividing the kingdom was a symbol of something much bigger, of prophecies that would soon be fulfilled. A new goddess would lead the world into a new era.

King Dimon and his army ranged around his disconnected territories, determined to unite Pangea once more. He rallied those whose possessions had all been engulfed by the waters of the rift. He suppressed rebellions and seized troublemakers who were stirring up civil unrest. He had unruly princes and minor kings thrown in chains and sent back to the city.

And thus it was that the rebel leader Urchin appeared on the scene. After a siege lasting many weeks, he admitted defeat and surrendered his domain to the king. Vicious bloodhounds chased him to the sea, seals towed him across the ocean on a barge, and finally he crawled, footsore, all the way to the palace gates to join a group of defeated princes and rebel leaders. They were herded together and shown into the chamber where the eternal princess lay in her casket. The princes knelt awestruck before her beauty and understood right away that Dimon possessed mysterious and powerful forces. They crouched down and murmured:

"Forgive me for my insurrection, eternal princess, don't let the god of thunder punish my people."

"She won't forgive you unless you cover the casket in gold," Gunnhild said firmly.

Obediently, the princes pulled the rings from their fingers and set them on the casket along with any other valuables they had. Urchin stood by, calmly waiting; when the princes had finished making their offerings and the guards had dragged them off to the dungeons, he drew from his leather pouch an enormous diamond, the largest Exel had ever seen.

Urchin bowed deeply and deferentially, saying: "I am Zee Urchin, heir of the great Urchin family of the East. I instigated a trivial little rebellion, but I now see that it was all a misunderstanding. It is a true honor to be subject once more to the dominion of Pangea."

He smiled, flashing his snow-white teeth. He appeared mesmerized by the casket, and tears flowed down his cheeks as he placed his hands on its lid. He closed his eyes and seemed to be about to pray, but instead said in a trembling voice:

"It feels as if she wants to say something."

"What?" said Gunnhild.

"Yes," said Urchin. "She is trying to make contact." He handed his diamond to Exel.

"Make contact?" said Exel, weighing the jewel in his palm.

"Yes!" Urchin closed his eyes, held his hands over the casket lid, and fell to his knees. "Yes! Forgive me, your Royal Highness. Forgive me for the rebellion. I did not mean to defy your father. I beg you not to be mad at me. I understand now! I understand! I have learned my lesson."

Exel watched him closely.

"The gods are not happy," said Urchin as if in a trance. "The princess is in a golden hall talking to the gods; they tell her that the people are concealing their riches. They could sacrifice so much more."

"More?" said Exel.

Urchin's eyes were closed and his body twitched. This was clearly a huge effort for him. "I can't do this." He trembled and his voice suddenly changed and became shrill and childlike. His eyes opened, staring wide, only the whites visible, as he shrieked at Gunnhild, "I am not pleased with you!"

Gunnhild started back in fear. "Oh? Why not? What have I done?"

"Because . . . because . . ." He wiped the sweat from his forehead. After a little while he recovered his composure. "I lost the connection," he said.

"What did she say?" said Gunnhild, pale as death. "I have looked after her well, kept the lid clean and polished the sides!"

"She is not getting enough. She needs more sacrifices to help support her father's crusade! He needs more time, more provisions, more reinforcements."

Exel, who was very familiar with the black hole in the royal accounts, pricked up his ears.

"She wants grander living quarters," Urchin went on. "She deserves to be placed where more people can gather to worship her. She needs a temple, and she knows what it should look like. Give me a pen! Quick! Quick!"

"Fetch a pen and paper!" yelled Exel.

Urchin pointed at the diamond and said: "If you return my diamond to me and give me more I can start construction tomorrow."

He sketched the outlines of a building. Exel and Gunnhild looked at him with suspicion, but Urchin added quickly: "And bring me a ball and chains. Obsidiana is angry with me. I may communicate her thoughts, but she demands that I should be permanently shackled."

Soon the temple dedicated to the Eternal Princess began to take shape. Birds held up golden bands to mark the outlines of the building. Elephants struggled under the weight of timber and marble. Artists decorated the walls. All the finest materials were ordered from the farthest corners of the world. Urchin was in charge of the project, wearing a golden cloak with two closed eyes embroidered on the chest. Heavy shackles weighed him down, and four strongmen had to carry him around the construction site.

Thordis sat next to the casket cuddling the panda. She thought about the little girl she had looked after, and how she missed her. Time passed slowly, like viscous, black tar. She thought about the day when she became Obsidiana's nurse; the day when the king's envoys knocked on her door and escorted her to the palace to breastfeed the princess. She knew that she would never be able to return home and see her own baby again. She had focused all her love and warmth on this girl, and now her sense of loss hit her with redoubled intensity.

It was cold. Snow covered the cherry trees, and Thordis would have loved to show Obsidiana how prettily the snowflakes were falling. When was the last time she had seen snow? But a gentle snowfall was not sufficient reason to disturb the princess's rest. And yet Thordis felt a sense of anticipation; soon there would be a new year—maybe she would be able to see Obsidiana then.

Snow fell, and the new year arrived punctually, as it had done from the beginning of time. The king was still far away. Guards marched in, shouldered the casket and carried it into the ceremonial hall, where everybody sat at a long table laden with the choicest foods. But the casket remained closed. It stood on a special plinth, like a decoration. Obsidiana's gentle smile made Thordis feel sad.

"How wonderful it is that she can be with us on New Year's Eve," Urchin said. His chains clinked beneath his golden cloak as he patted the lid of the casket. "Such a sweet and obedient girl, a friend of the gods."

Exel came striding across the hall, unhesitating and confident—he didn't have to worry about stepping on lines anymore because the floors of the palace had been relaid and were now smooth and seamless. He proudly began to itemize all the offerings that people had brought to Obsidiana since Urchin had started to interpret her thoughts.

"An increase of 457%," he said. "And we expect at least as much again when the temple is completed." The maids and the men wearing suits patterned like graph paper all applauded warmly. Urchin rose to his feet and, putting his hands on the lid of the casket, closed his eyes and said with a smile: "The immortal princess is happy today, and she graces us with her warmest greetings." His eyes rolled back in his head as he said in a high-pitched girl's voice, "Happy new year, dear family. I bring you greetings from the gods."

This was too much for Thordis, who jumped to her feet and said, "The dwarfs never said anything about a connection to the gods, and Princess Obsidiana has never spoken of it! They warned us about the casket!"

"How dare you dispute her divine connection!" Exel shouted. "The Eternal Princess is Pangea's heart. Dimon would have long since run out of weapons and supplies if it hadn't been for the offerings that the people have brought to her. She came to us at a moment of destiny."

With a lump in her throat, Thordis said: "Can we not allow her out for a while? It is New Year's Eve, after all."

Exel said dryly: "Surely you would not want her to be needlessly upset by the absence of her father? Would you be prepared to tell her that the king is far north of the seven mountains and the twelve deserts?"

Thordis fell silent. She gazed down at her plate and didn't know what to do with herself.

Urchin now spoke. "Why is this woman here?" he demanded, pointing at Thordis. He turned to the assembled company. "Does she have noble blood in her veins? I wear shackles though I am born of nobility. Can we afford to employ a nursemaid with nothing to do? Footmen! Here is a discontented woman who needs a job!"

A footman handed Thordis a wooden spoon and led her down to the kitchens. Through the crystal-clear spider's silk of the casket you could see the mysterious, frozen smile on Obsidiana's lips. Observing her, the servants couldn't help thinking: *why doesn't she ask the gods for help when her nursemaid is being sent in tears down to the kitchen?*

The temple towered over the square, clad in gleaming black marble, steel, and fine glass. In a daily ritual, Obsidiana was carried across the square and into the temple with an escort led by Urchin. Inside, an endless line of pilgrims waited with their offerings and urgent problems for her to solve. Rich and poor, they murmured their prayers and touched the casket's lid in the hope of finding cures for rheumatism, polio, lung diseases, madness, leprosy, and tuberculosis; every citizen was expected to touch the casket at least once during their lifetime. Occasionally an old red panda could be seen sitting mournfully on the roof of the temple.

So the days passed, and the cherry orchards became pink, then faded, and then pink again, while the sleepless king led his troops and herds of animals through forests and swamps, in cold and hot weather, along the entire length of the rift, in his never-ending struggle to keep his empire together.

Obsidiana continued to smile her sweet smile, oblivious of all the years that had passed since the king had departed, and unaware that her dear, kind Nursie was peeling potatoes in a damp basement.

It had been a bright, sunny day when her father closed the casket all that time ago and took his leave of her saying, "Two years for me; only a moment for you, my love."

The casket opened again a moment later, or so it seemed to Obsidiana. The night was pitch-dark and a cold breeze brushed her face. Her eyes tried to adjust to the darkness. *Has Papa returned?* she thought. But before she could utter a word, small hands appeared out of the darkness, clasped her throat, and tried to strangle her.

Fighting the Monster

I t was the middle of the night and a faint glimmer of moon-light shone into the room. Obsidiana fought to catch her breath, but the unknown creature tightened its grip. At last she managed to give the thing a hard kick and it fell with a thump to the floor. Obsidiana jumped to her feet and looked around. Barefoot, she carefully stepped onto the cold marble as if expecting there to be broken glass or some animal about to nip her toes. She crept around the casket, her heart pounding, and stopped to listen for anyone coming up behind her.

"Who's there?" she whispered. She wanted to scream but was too scared. Something dark, like a little imp, darted past her and disappeared behind the thick drapes in the corner. *What devil was trying to strangle me?* she thought. Quickly collecting herself, she felt her neck, and discovered that her necklace was gone—her mother's necklace! Now she was mad. She shot over to the corner. She heard a rustling noise and just managed to grab a foot that was in the process of squeezing through a small hole in the panel behind the drapes. She dragged the creature back into the room as if it were her own shadow, but the shadow turned and attacked her. She caught a flash of the necklace and grabbed the hand clutching it, but the beast was as lithe as a cat and bit the back of her hand. Obsidiana yelled in pain. She caught hold of a corner of her assailant's mouth and tugged it back across its cheek, only to get a sharp kick in the back. She howled but managed to grab a handful of tangled hair. With a piteous wail the creature stopped fighting. Seizing the opportunity, Obsidiana straddled it and pinned it to the floor. She found herself looking down at the dirty face of a little boy, who grimaced and tried to struggle free. She slapped his face, and he tried to retaliate with his free hand so she yelled: "GUARDS! GUARDS!"

Panicking, the boy sobbed: "No! Please don't shout!"

She could feel the heart pounding like a trapped bird in the boy's chest.

His breath came in gasps as she yelled again: "GUARDS! GUARDS! HELP!"

The boy began to cry. "They'll kill me!" He gazed imploringly at Obsidiana and whispered, "Don't call, they'll kill me!"

"No, they won't kill you."

"Yes they will, believe me!"

There was no sign of the guards. They must be fast asleep out in the corridor.

"You little devil. You were going to steal my necklace. The necklace my mother gave me! It would serve you right if they did kill you!"

She slapped him again, this time really hard; she felt he deserved much more.

But he didn't fight back; he just continued to sob. Still she held him down, but she could tell that he had stopped resisting.

"Stop crying. You're just a kid. They don't kill little kids. They'll just tell you off."

"They so will kill me!"

"No, they'll just send you home."

"They'll kill everybody there, too!" he said. Obsidiana looked around and tried to work out where she was. She gazed across at the west window, through which she could see an ocean and a beach stretched out beneath a full moon.

"Where are we?" she asked. The room was as she remembered it except that now there were gold mosaic pictures on the ceiling: pictures of dwarfs and a magic casket, pictures of her, and pictures of gods.

"We're in the palace," the boy said.

"What's that sound?"

"It's the waves."

"Waves?" She listened more intently. Somebody was wailing outside and she shuddered; it sounded like a baby crying.

"Who's that wailing?"

"It's the gulls."

Gulls? she thought. She had never seen gulls. She peered out over the ocean. It looked like an enormous, dark mirror.

"Where does all this water come from?"

"It's the sea. It came when the rift happened, and the kingdom split apart."

She tried to understand what he was saying, while still keeping a firm hold of him.

"What's your name?"

"Anori."

She noticed that he kept an eye on the door; he was trembling. "Who sent you here?"

"Nobody."

"Did some kind of mobsters send you?"

"No, I just came by myself," he said, hesitantly.

"What season is it?"

"It's spring."

"What spring?"

"Just spring! I don't know what spring!"

"Where's my father?"

"People say he's away."

"Where?"

"In the war in the west, of course!"

"Is it a big war? How long has he been away for?"

"I don't know. All I know is, my dad was sent to fight after the battle with the Albitricians on the Great Plains."

"Is your dad a soldier?"

"Yes, he's the strongest soldier in the whole world."

"Oh, is he now? Does he know you broke into the palace?"

"He was sent to the war before I was born. I've never seen him. Mom is poor, so I've been living with my great-aunt Borghild since Dad left."

Listening to Anori, Obsidiana tried to piece the world together. Did the kingdom split apart? This ocean, this never-ending body of water—where had it come from? The boy tried to twist himself out of her grasp, but she gripped his wrists tightly.

"What year is it?"

"I don't know."

"How long have I been in the casket?"

"I don't know—since forever. I just came across an old tunnel and then I discovered this room and saw the necklace and decided to take it. I didn't know you could talk. I didn't know you could move. Please don't let the gods punish me."

Obsidiana looked at him. "Gods punish you? Why do you say that?"

Anori looked at her. She who knew the gods better than anybody pretended she didn't know anything.

Obsidiana rubbed her eyes. The city she had known since she was a child and longed to get to know better was but half its original size; it ended at the stadium, which was only half an amphitheater now. The western hills and the Seven Towers that had stood there were nowhere to be seen—there was nothing there aside from the moon and the ocean smooth as a mirror.

The palace was utterly silent. *Nobody is going to come*, she thought, but her fear subsided as she recognized she was stronger than the boy. She continued to pin him down.

"I'll make a deal with you," she said. "And if you agree, then I won't call the guards."

The boy nodded.

"Can I trust you?"

"Yes."

"I'll let you go if you promise to tell me what's happening in the world and show me where you came from."

"Okay. But what about the gods?"

"What about them?"

"Will they punish me?"

Strange child, she thought. *Keeps talking about the gods*. She looked into his eyes, "Of course not. If you trust me, then I'll trust you. Do we have a deal?" Carefully, she relaxed her hold. "I'll let go of you now if you promise not to do anything."

"I promise."

Obsidiana released him, expecting a counter-attack; but the boy remained calm. He sat on the floor, exhausted, and rubbed his wrists. They both sat silent for a good while. Obsidiana looked at this little kid with his grimy face and unkempt hair, his clothes crumpled and patched. He would never have passed Exel's friendship test, but if nobody was prepared to help her get friends, she would find them herself.

The Tower

Anori showed Obsidiana a loose panel hidden behind the drapes; he pushed it aside and she felt a cold breeze on her face. She watched as Anori moved first one piece of wood, then another, then a third; there was a sharp click and he carefully reached to one side to release a small bolt and open a hatch. An icy chill greeted them. Anori crawled ahead and Obsidiana warily followed. Portholes in the masonry let in a hint of moonlight; it was drafty, there was a smell of ancient damp and mold, and a spider's web got tangled in her hair. Before she knew it, they had arrived in a back room that she had never seen before. Obsidiana peered into an abyss and saw a spiral staircase disappearing down into the darkness.

"Watch your step!" said Anori.

She stared downward, her heart thumping. "I've never been here," she said, gazing into the darkness that echoed beneath her feet. "Does anyone else know how to get into my room?"

"No."

"Are you sure?"

"Last year a thief got into the vaults and then up into the castle. He was hanged in the square."

"I don't believe you. Thieves don't get hanged." Anori shook his head. She was odd, this girl. "They bricked over the opening he used, but I found this way."

She tried to gauge whether he was telling the truth. "You say some strange things," she said.

"You say some strange things yourself. Actually, it's strange that you speak at all."

"It's not strange that I speak! It's strange that you find it strange that I speak!"

She wasn't scared anymore. For the first time in her life nobody was watching her. No guards stood by, and for the first time she knew that there was a way out. She would be able to explore the world.

"Downward from here the staircase leads to a mine, but upward it leads to an abandoned watchtower," Anori said. Most of the stairs were missing; he stepped across the void and had to hang onto the staircase's central column as he edged himself slowly upward using whatever footing he could get from small projections and the remains of broken steps.

"Wait!" said Obsidiana. She slipped off her overdress and placed it carefully in a dry place. Then she embraced the column, found a handhold and felt her way upward. She had to hold on tight and get used to the idea that if she were to fall there wouldn't be any guards there ready to catch her with a silk rug.

They clambered upward until the stairs became sound again. They ascended in endless shell-like spirals—up and up until they stepped out at last onto an abandoned, flat-roofed watchtower. Torches burned on poles in many places throughout the city. They heard singing in some distant inn. A woman shouted at her husband. Carriages clattered loudly along cobbled streets, and they heard the crying of children woken by the noise, and the shouts of women cursing the carriage drivers. She closed her eyes and inhaled a dense smell of firewood, bread baking, and meat frying, mingled with the stench of sewers.

"I've never been up here," she said, enthralled.

"I live over there," said Anori, pointing at a cluster of what looked more or less like hovels clinging to a rocky height.

"Will you show me the city?" she asked.

"No, you can't go into town with me."

"Why do you say that?"

"You always have an escort of guards when you go there."

"No, I've never been into the city!"

He looked at her, trying to figure her out. How could she say this? She was carried there every single day!

"But if I'm in disguise I can go anywhere," she said. She had dreamed up a hundred disguises for herself when she was trying to think of a way to sneak outside and meet the kids playing beyond the castle walls.

Anori pondered this. "Maybe later," he said.

"What about the sea? Can I see the sea?"

"Later." All at once he went quiet, listening intently.

"What?"

"I heard something." He seemed scared. From the watchtower there was a view over the palace gardens to the ivory tower where Obsidiana had been born and her mother had died. Obsidiana gazed out at the sea, at its silvery, mirrorlike gleam. The seagulls wailed. On the square in front of the castle was an unfamiliar building decorated with gold.

"What's that building?" she asked.

"It's your temple!" Anori said.

Not wanting to sound stupid, she said, "Oh yes, of course. It's just that I haven't seen it from this angle before." She stared in amazement at the building, with its marble columns and golden roof. She puzzled over this, realizing that it must have taken some years to build. Suddenly she became anxious.

"What year is it now? Tell me about time," she said. Just then they heard soldiers marching.

"They're changing the guard," said Anori and looked around. "I can't stay here any longer. I have to go."

They retraced their steps to her room, where she hurriedly put her dress back on, dusted herself down, and jumped back into the casket. They could hear movement outside and fell completely silent.

Anori shook with fear. "I have to go," he whispered.

"You must promise to come back and tell me about the world!"

He rubbed his wrists and thought about this. "When shall I come back?"

"Come next time we can see by the light of the silvery moon."

"How can I trust you?" he said. "You could have me arrested!"

"How can I trust *you*?" she retorted.

He looked at her, his eyes as dark as the night. "I promise," he said.

Obsidiana offered him her hand, and they shook on the deal. She lay back in the casket and Anori carefully closed the lid. Obsidiana went rigid, as if she were dead, and the moonlight gave her complexion a faint tinge of blue. *That's really strange*, thought Anori, and gingerly reopened the casket.

"Hi, Anori! Do you bring news from the world of time?" said Obsidiana with a smile.

"I just wanted to say bye," he said, closing the lid again. He looked at her and giggled—one eye was half-closed, her mouth was crooked, and she looked as scary as a ghost. He opened the casket again.

"You're back?"

"No, your face was so funny. You have to look just like you did when I opened the casket. Smile!"

She smiled, and he quickly shut the lid to preserve her expression. Sounds came from the corridor and somebody fiddled with the lock and door-catch. Anori darted through the hole behind the drapes and left the castle the same way he had come. As he emerged into the alleyway outside he looked around furtively; there was nobody about, and he ran along the cobbled streets all the way home.

Anori's Hovel

Anori tossed and turned. He was up on the roof where he slept in the summer when it was too hot to sleep indoors. He lay awake listening to the crickets and the yapping of stray dogs fighting. He stared up at the starry sky, deep and endless, thinking about the warning words of his aunt Borghild, who was snoring downstairs:

"Don't go anywhere near the palace. The guards are vicious. They could kill you just for the fun of it. Don't draw attention to yourself, don't carry your head high, and don't pretend to be strong. Don't fight back—better to let others beat you up, otherwise they'll recruit you into the army."

Anori closed his eyes. He had met the Eternal Princess. She had spoken to him, and she wanted to meet him again.

A kick in the ribs woke him. He hardly dared open his eyes. A bunch of roughnecks loomed over him, and one of them dragged him violently to his feet.

"You gave us the slip! Wasn't there anything in that hole? We waited more than two hours."

"No," said Anori, shaking from head to toe. "I went everywhere. I got lost and couldn't find the way out."

"That's a shit excuse. What did you find?"

"It was just an old rabbit hole. There was nothing there, not even an old rabbit."

They stared at him threateningly.

"You hiding something?"

"No," Anori said, trembling. "I didn't find nothing!"

One of them grabbed him by the ear and twisted it. "You cheat on us, you know what happens!"

"Yes!" Anori wailed. They hauled him out and shoved him ahead of them down the stairs. They came out into a narrow alleyway. Rats darted about among the garbage and filth. They pointed at a window on the third floor.

"There's a merchant lives up there. He's out of town fetching stuff. Get yourself up there and empty the place!"

Anori didn't dare disobey. He shimmied up a climbing plant and slipped through a window into a parlor with ornate rugs on the floors and walls. He could hear snoring sounds coming from an adjacent room. He moved around silently, tiptoeing like a cat. He grabbed a silver plate and a golden candlestick. There was a secret compartment with a bag of gold coins in it, and he also found a beautiful sword, decorated with precious stones. Looking around the room he couldn't see anything else worth stealing. This had only taken a brief moment. He felt relieved. It was a decent haul, so maybe they'd leave him in peace, at least for a while.

"Cool," said the leader of the gang. "Follow me." He gave a low whistle and a guy appeared leading some horses; they sat Anori on one of them and rode out of the city. Anori's stomach tightened when he realized they were heading for the forbidden valley where noblemen and royalties lay buried in grass-covered graves. Frogs croaked, and the wind sang in the reeds. They rode on until they met two men carrying shovels and picks. Close by they saw a man lying tied up in the grass. *The graveyard attendant*, Anori thought.

Deep in the hole that the men had dug was a small opening; one of the bandits pointed at it. Knowing what was expected of him, Anori climbed down and poked his head through the opening. Gagging at the unbearable stench, he nevertheless felt his way in the dark along the cracked marble floor. He forced himself not to think about the dead people, who were said to latch onto grave robbers and keep them in their clutches for eternity. He detected a lifeless, shriveled hand and felt it all over until he found a ring, which he tried to slip past the knucklebone; but the whole finger fell off, so he broke it in two, got the ring off, and crept on his way through the blackness. The air was heavy and smelled like the pile of entrails behind a slaughterhouse. He found an earring and a small jewelry box, and he stuck his fingers into the mouth of a gaping skull looking for a gold tooth. He retched, his stomach was heaving, and the stench grew still stronger; someone had obviously been buried recently. He felt his way onward. He stumbled on a corpse that was crawling with bugs. Anori shrieked and backed out. *Yikes! Flaming carrion beetles!* The gang gave him a torch to light his way and shoved him back in again, telling him to finish the job. Something bit his leg, stinging him like nettles. Anori screamed. He closed his sack and scrambled back out, shuddering and beating the bugs from his sleeves. Five guys were waiting for him in the dark with cloths covering their noses and mouths. The tallest one—Anori noticed he had a finger missing—snatched the sack from him.

"Is this all?"

"Yes," Anori muttered.

One of the others grabbed him and forced his mouth open to see if he was concealing a ring or a diamond, and then felt him all over.

"Just as well," he said. "You made us wait way too long last time!"

"I got lost," said Anori. "I could have died in there."

"You took too long. You're getting nothing this time!"

"Other than the curses of the dead!" another said, laughing sarcastically.

The gang rode off, leaving Anori scowling and spitting after them. He never knew when to expect them; they would just turn up out of the blue and drag him away. He didn't know where they came from, but he wished they would die. He regretted having given them the sword. He wanted to stab them all to death with it. His dad would give them such a beating when he returned from the war!

Anori finally got back to his bed just as the sun was rising; cockerels were crowing all over the city, and it was warm. He wrapped himself in a thin blanket and listened to his aunt's gentle snoring.

The next days and weeks seemed like an eternity. Borghild kept finding jobs for him to do. He had to get firewood from the forest, plant the little yard, feed the pig, and spread the washing out on a rock. All the while his mind was soaring, thinking of the princess in the casket. Nobody he knew had heard her speak.

One day, when the sound of bells echoing around the city told him that the monks were taking her to the temple, he ran through the streets, the crowds growing denser and denser, until the glorious temple came into view. Men and women thrust themselves forward with their sacrifices and gifts, but Anori slipped past them in the line. People bombarded him with angry words in incomprehensible languages; thousands had gathered here from all over to touch the casket. Peddlers wandered around selling bread, water, and holy objects, and the guards ensured that everybody made an offering of some kind. Anori had managed to sneak unseen into the brewery to steal a handful of grain. This would have kept his belly full for two whole days, but he was determined to see the girl in the casket.

The line moved slowly nearer. At last he saw Obsidiana, smiling exactly as she had been when he closed the casket that night. He stood there lost in his thoughts until a guard poked him: "MOVE ON! MOVE ON!"

Carried along with the crowd, he looked back over his shoulder. It seemed so strange that she was able to live and talk. For a moment he felt a surge of pride that he knew her and that she had asked him to come back—the Eternal Princess, who was worshipped by the whole world. He glimpsed the necklace, felt shame and begged her silently not to let the gods punish him: "Eternal Princess, I promise to come back. Kind princess, please tell those bullies to leave me in peace."

Now Zee Urchin, the court chaplain, appeared. He was enormously tall and wore a golden tunic bearing strange lettering; diamonds adorned his headpiece, and embroidered on his chest were two closed eyes, the emblem of the Eternal Princess. Heavy gold chains shackled him. He was followed by massive strongmen, dressed in blue. He approached the plinth on which the casket lay and put both his hands on the lid. He closed his eyes and chanted, and then his eyes opened wide and he cried out in a strange accent from the north:

"Blessed be the Eternal Princess and blessed be the gods she dwells among! Your sacrifices are not for nothing. They will await you in the form of riches after death. Approach and fill the heavenly coffers!"

The strongmen now led forward a stout man with a black eye, who looked as if someone had beaten him up and rolled him in the dirt.

"King Dimon has confronted great adversities! It is his resolve to reunite the kingdom of Pangea, and he has won many victories in pursuit of that aim. In order to achieve his goal, he needs everyone to contribute grains, weapons, and cloth. But this man standing here, though he possesses huge stores of wheat, has sacrificed none of it! This man has hoarded all his wealth. The Eternal Princess sent me a dream revealing his hiding place. The gods have decided on a fitting punishment. He will be thrown into the rift!"

The man grew pale. A woman in the audience wailed.

Urchin shouted, "Humble yourselves before the princess and worship!" Everybody prostrated themselves, Anori included. He trembled and feared the same fate—that the Eternal Princess would tell the gods he was a thief, and demand punishment.

Full Moon

Anori kept an anxious eye on the moon, following its phases as it waned and waxed. Much to his relief, the gang was nowhere to be seen—maybe the princess had answered his prayers after all. He took his role seriously and set about getting news from the world of time. He went to the grocery store and asked:

"What news is there of the king and the war?"

The grocer looked at him in amazement. "Scram!"

Anori ran off in fear. He met an old man and asked: "What year is it?"

"Do you mean the old calendar or the new one?"

"The new one."

"The new calendar hasn't begun yet. Not until the king has reunited Pangea."

"When will that happen?"

The old man looked intently at the boy. "You know the king is waging a war on time. People who ask too many questions come to a sticky end. Mark my words—the walls have ears."

When Anori got home he asked his aunt, "Why do the walls have ears?"

"For the same reason a john has no nose," Borghild said.

"The old man said the walls have ears."

She put down her knitting, looked around and whispered: "Why did he say that?"

"I just asked him what year it was."

"You're not supposed to ask questions like that, child! What's brought this on?"

"I need to know how King Dimon is doing in the war, and when he's coming back."

"Hush! You'll put us in danger if you keep on with nonsense like that. If anybody asks you the answer's simple: The war is going very well, Dimon is the greatest king in the world, he is going to reunite Pangea, and that's the end of that!"

Anori tried to wish the moon along faster. At last there came a clear, bright night and he snuck back to the rabbit hole that led into the mine and under the palace. His head was full of all the horrible things that could happen to him as he fumbled his way in the darkness up the spiral staircase and into the back room. His stomach was tied in knots as he poked his head through the hole in the paneling and saw Obsidiana lying bathed in moonlight. He heard the murmuring of waves, the wind in the trees, and an occasional seagull's wail. He crept across to the door and listened for movement outside. His heart was pounding as he approached the casket and carefully lifted the lid. Obsidiana opened her eyes.

"What?" she whispered.

"What do you mean, what?" he asked.

"Aren't you going to go home?"

Anori blushed. "Go home? I've only just arrived!"

She looked around and screwed up her eyes. "Oh, is there another new moon now?"

"Yes."

"Sorry," she said, jumping out of the casket. "Sometimes I'm a little mixed up."

They snuck into the back room. As soon as they felt safe,

Obsidiana said: "So tell me, Anori, what's the news from the world of time?"

Anori thought. "My pig ate the neighbor's cap!"

"No," she said and laughed. "Tell me about the king. What year is it now? I need to know."

Anori had memorized what his aunt had said. "The war is going very well, Dimon is the greatest king in the world, he is going to reunite Pangea."

"Yes, but what else do you know? What time is it? What year is it now?"

Anori wasn't sure what to say. "I did ask people about it. I think that now is an in-between time. The new calendar won't begin until the king comes back."

"In-between time? So when will the king come back?"

"They say the war is going well."

"But how long have I been here?"

Again, Anori had to think.

"Since the olden days. A hundred years, maybe more!"

That shocked her at first, but she quickly did some mental calculations.

"That can't be right, silly! My father would have died of old age."

Anori scratched his head. "Well, maybe not a hundred, but at least longer than I've been alive."

Obsidiana looked at him. He was smaller than she was by a head. This time, he had obviously combed his hair and washed his face.

"Tell me about the rift. How did it happen?"

"The Great Rift was here before I was born."

"What happened?"

"My aunt told me the story when I was little."

"Tell it to me!"

"Okay. The king loved his daughter so much that he wanted her to live forever. He promised half the kingdom to anybody who could bring her more time. Magicians and sorcerers came, but nobody could capture time for him. Then one day some dwarfs arrived in the capital city of Pangea with an eternity casket."

"I remember this!" she said. "But it sounds like a real fairy tale!"

"Oh! So you know the story; I don't need to tell it to you."

"No, carry on! I want to hear it the way you heard it."

"Well, the casket was a true magic casket, and it preserved the beauty of the princess. The king was going to give half the kingdom to the dwarfs, but they wouldn't accept it. The king grew mad and ordered their heads chopped off in the stadium. When the ax fell on the last dwarf it opened a rift in the ground and the kingdom split into two."

"Is that it?" said Obsidiana disappointedly.

"Yes."

"That's complete nonsense! The dwarfs weren't beheaded; they went back to their home. And you can't split a whole country with an ax. Who tells you this stuff?"

Anori swallowed nervously. "I'm sorry," he said. "My aunt told it me. Please don't punish her."

"I'm not going to punish anyone. It's just that the story simply isn't true."

Anori fell silent. Obsidiana saw that he was shaken. "Forgive me," she said and patted his hand. "Of course you can tell me stories. But I need to understand what is happening in the world. I need to know how long I've been here. Please come again and open the casket to let me back into time; and tell me stories—all the ones you know."

He went home and listened to what people said about goings-on in the city but was able to glean precious little information—certainly, nobody was prepared to tell him anything about what Obsidiana was longing to know. He tried, nevertheless, to invent at least one new story to tell at each new moon.

If he heard too much noise coming from the guards, he would just open the casket's lid a tiny crack and whisper: "The guards are right outside," and then sneak away. But sometimes they sat together all through the night, chatting.

"What else do you know?"

"My aunt saw the country split apart. Her sweetheart was picking flowers for her when the ground split between them. They watched each other moving farther and farther apart for months on end, he with faded flowers in his hand. She wept when the land disappeared over the horizon."

"How sad," said Obsidiana, and fell silent. "Do you have friends?" she said.

"Yes, there are lots of kids living on my street. What about you? What are your friends called?"

She had to think carefully about this. "They're called Peak and Moon."

"Strange names."

"They're deer, silly! Also, I used to have a panda, but it went away. One day I'll show you my garden. It has a pond and there's a funny old man called Jako. He is also my friend even if he's old. He is very clever."

They sat silent for a while, but it wasn't an uncomfortable silence. Obsidiana thought about a proverb that Jako had taught her once: "It's good to be silent with a friend."

"Do you want to hear more stories?" Anori asked.

112

"The story of your aunt was sad, and the story about the dwarfs was just plain nonsense," Obsidiana said. "Tell me a story that has a good ending."

Anori had been planning to tell Obsidiana about animals—how the city was once full of animals that helped the people, but then they were sent to fight the king's war. But that story was also sad. How was it that she wanted to know all about the world and yet didn't want to know anything?

"Once upon a time there lived an ogre under a bridge. Three tasty goats wanted to cross the bridge. The kid went first and the ogre said: 'Now I'm going to eat you.' But the kid said: 'Don't eat me. Why don't you eat my mom, she is bigger and fatter than I am.' The ogre was totally shocked by this unfaithful kid. Did he want his mother to be eaten so his life could be spared? The puzzled ogre sat and waited for the mother to cross. The mother goat said: 'Don't eat me, why don't you eat my husband? He's bigger and fatter than I am.' This made the ogre completely lose his appetite. 'What's the world coming to?' he cried. 'The kid tells me to eat his mother and then she tells me to eat the billy goat. What a family!'"

Obsidiana shook her head. "And what happened to the ogre?"

"He went back home, just like the dwarfs," Anori said with a shrug.

"Well, at least this story had a happy ending," Obsidiana said, and giggled.

Each time they closed the casket they were careful to make sure that Obsidiana had the same look on her face and that her dress was draped the same way as before. But there was always a slight difference. Wise women noticed that after every new moon the look on her face changed. If she looked happy, good times lay ahead; an inscrutable expression meant uncertainty. If her fist was clenched, there would be hard times.

A Year in a Single Night

Anori had just started one of his stories when Obsidiana suddenly told him to stop.

"What?" said Anori.

She peered at him, trying to get a better look at him in the dark. Every time they met he had changed. He was getting taller.

"I don't know how to talk about time."

"How do you mean?"

"You've been coming to see me for a whole year. But to me that year has been just one long moonlit night. Four seasons have passed in a single night."

Anori tried to see it from her point of view, but he was finding it difficult.

"I feel like I got to know you only yesterday," she went on, "but you've known me for a whole year. All that time, nobody else has come to see me. No one! I need to know what has happened. Where is my nurse? Where is my father? Where is everyone? Last time I knew, I'd had sixteen birthdays. Now another whole year has passed, and nobody celebrated my birthday."

"Of course there was a birthday," Anori said. "There was a festival on the city square."

"There was? But I wasn't invited."

"But you liked your presents. That's what Urchin said."

"Urchin? Who's Urchin?"

"Zee Urchin, the court chaplain!"

Obsidiana shook her head. "I've never heard anybody mention him."

Anori was baffled; Urchin and Obsidiana had appeared together on the square as far back as he could remember.

There was a sudden plaintive sound like a cat meowing. Obsidiana clutched her stomach and doubled up in pain. "Are you alright?" Anori asked.

"It really, really hurts!" she said. She could hardly move. The pain worsened, and she broke into tears.

Anori was scared. "Are you alright? Are you ill?"

"Listen to that noise," she whimpered. "I think I may be dying!"

Anori put his ear to her stomach and giggled: "It's your tummy rumbling! How long is it since you last had a meal? You're obviously hungry!"

"Hungry?" she groaned. He had been here twelve times and she hadn't eaten anything since their first meeting.

Anori shook his head. "Have you never been hungry?"

"Not like this."

"I know where the kitchen is."

"How do you know that?"

"Never mind," he said. It was no coincidence that he'd grown so fast. "I found a secret tunnel that leads down to the pantry. It'll take us past the guards."

Like phantoms they slipped through the castle, hidden behind the paneling. As they passed, Obsidiana pointed through a small hole in the wall: "This is where everybody sleeps," she whispered. "There's my garden and my room." Suddenly one of the panels creaked, and through a knothole they saw a lady-in-waiting running from the room as if she had seen a ghost.

They found the pantry. It was stacked with delicious food—whole carcasses of smoked meat were suspended from metal hooks; antelopes' heads, sacks of grain, and piles of cheese filled every shelf. They stole some bread and milk and found some sausages, a large piece of cheese, and a bowlful of apples, which they put into a sack and carried back to the watchtower. They sat down and eagerly munched the food. Anori burped. Obsidiana giggled and burped too. Above them the stars and the moon shone. She yawned.

"I'm tired," she said.

"Tired?" he said indignantly. "You're always asleep!"

"No, you go home to sleep, but I go into the casket and that's not sleep."

"So what happens?"

"Nothing. Nothing happens. As soon as you close the casket it immediately opens again."

"Not even dreams?"

"No, nothing."

"I see," he said, not really seeing at all. "But what about the gods?"

"The gods?"

"They say that when you're in the casket, your soul goes to the gods. That's why you always stay the same."

Obsidiana shook her head. "What nonsense! Who told you this? I'm just here. I don't go anywhere."

"So my dad won't come back, then?" he asked.

"Why do you ask me that?"

"I gave you a handful of grain and asked you to help my dad get back home."

"When was this?"

"Last year."

"I don't remember that. I don't even know where *my* dad is!"

Anori looked disappointed. Obsidiana snuggled up against his shoulder and fell asleep. He sat listening to the crickets and passed the time poking at ants and flies or jabbing a stick into the gaps between the flagstones, before he too dozed off. When the screams of seagulls woke them, the sun was already coming up. Obsidiana nudged Anori. She took a good look at him in the daylight. In the short time she'd known him he had grown like a weed before her eyes; he'd lost his baby teeth and grown adult teeth; his nose had changed; and his hair had gotten longer and then shorter and then longer again.

"Let's go into town!" she said.

"No, we can't do that."

"I have to know what's happening in the world. We must go into town now!"

"We can't, you're about to go to the temple."

"No, I'm not going to the temple."

"Yes you are, they'll be coming for you at noon, and they'll carry you there."

"Why?"

"You pretend you don't know anything. You act as if you're stupid."

"No! I'm not stupid. If guards are coming for me at noon then we have three hours. The town is just nearby. I must go into town! I have to get there!"

Anori thought this over. He came to a decision. "The next time I come, we'll go into town."

"You promise?"

"Yes. The gods are with you, so it must be possible."

Off with Her Hand

Anori got things ready for the next full moon. When he came to wake Obsidiana he brought cloaks for them to wear and a veil to cover her face. They edged their way cautiously down the spiral staircase—far, far down into the long and winding passageways beneath the palace. A secret tunnel led out under the streets of the city. Anori opened an ancient door leading to the basement of an abandoned house that stood in a deserted alley. From there they made their way downtown to where the hustle and bustle of city life soon engulfed them. Obsidiana had never seen such crowds of people. Everywhere she was mesmerized by the shouting, haggling, shoving, and grafting. Old and young, men and women, camels, donkeys, and carriages all in a jumble. She breathed in an atmosphere that smelled of animals, spices and freshly baked bread. There were men with monkeys on chains, snakes in wicker baskets, chickens and rabbits. Flies buzzed around hunks of meat hanging from hooks. There were apples and mandarins, dates and nuts. A man took a knife and slit the throat of a goat on a counter in front of them, and Obsidiana shrieked and looked away. Beggars and lepers held out their skeletal fingers in supplication, children milled about everywhere, splashing in muddy puddles. Butchers shouted their wares, and blood from their trestles mingled with the mud underfoot where chickens ran hither and thither to avoid being trampled by the crush of people rushing by. Traders thrust their wares at her, teenage boys pinched her, and Anori pushed them all away. He was getting anxious; he took her hand and tried to move her on, saying:

"We mustn't stay long. Be sure you keep your face hidden."

But Obsidiana's eyes shone as she said to him: "Thank you Anori! Thank you for showing me the city!"

Obsidiana reveled in the scent of spices, the feel of silk, the kaleidoscope of colors—but suddenly she stopped in astonishment. There was a little altar, and in the middle of it was a golden icon of a girl in a blue dress lying in a glass casket.

An old woman with no teeth said: "Good price. I give you good price!"

That's me, Obsidiana thought, staring at the altar. The whole booth was dedicated to pictures of her: big pictures and small, statuettes, painted eggs and stones.

"See! This picture is good for you!" the old woman said, handing her an image.

"Thank you," said Obsidiana brightly, and looked around for Anori. He signaled for her to hurry. She ran over to him with the picture.

"Look what I got!" Anori saw the icon and grew pale.

"Where did you get this?"

"Over there," she said, pointing toward the booth, but it was too late—somebody shouted: "STOP THIEF!"

"Run!" shouted Anori and pulled her away. Hustlers and rug-sellers grabbed their knives and whips; the butcher took hold of his meat cleaver and headed off in pursuit. "Come on!" Anori yelled. "Run! They cut thieves' hands off!" Obsidiana ran for her life, but before she got far someone seized her by the shoulders and started shaking her.

Two wrinkled old women snarled at her. "Fief! Fief!" they shrieked through toothless gums, shoving her back and forth between them. The mob roared: "OFF WITH HER HAND!" and the thick-necked butcher brandished his cleaver. The women grasped Obsidiana's arm and pulled up her sleeves and someone brought a thick plank of wood to use as a block, as more people gathered shouting: "OFF WITH HER HAND! OFF WITH HER HAND!"

The butcher raised his cleaver and aimed it at her wrist. Obsidiana screamed at the top of her voice: "No! Please!"

An old woman ripped the veil off her: "Show your face, you scum!"

And there, exposed to their gaze, was that beautiful face— the face the world had worshipped, the hair that was black as a raven's wing, the lips red as blood. The mob fell silent. The women released their grip and hurriedly backed away. The butcher shrank. He became like a little mouse and then like a housefly. He flung himself to the ground and threw dirt over himself like a sparrow in a dust bath.

"The Eternal Princess is here," the people whispered. "The Eternal Princess is among us." They fell to the ground as if an earthquake had struck. They lay prostrate and chanted. Grown men wept. This was a miracle!

An old woman with a sick child in her arms approached Obsidiana; she muttered prayers and begged Obsidiana to touch the child. Obsidiana froze. The child was crooked and twisted and its head was too big. *Poor little person*, she thought and stroked the child gently on the cheek. She had never been near such a tiny thing. She gazed at it in amazement.

"Let's go!" Anori yelled. He yanked Obsidiana by the arm and pulled her after him.

They ran along streets filled with people prostrating them-selves, their bottoms in the air looking like hummocks on a

120

prairie. She was careful not to step on anybody's fingers or toes, but she heard someone yell behind her: "She touched me! I've been blessed!"

Obsidiana was bewildered. The city was carpeted with bodies chanting:

"THE ETERNAL PRINCESS! THE ETERNAL PRINCESS!"

The people lay so close together that she was forced to step on those with the broadest backs and biggest butts, and thus they jumped from one back to the next until they reached the alleyway and the rabbit hole. Once inside, they scampered through the darkness until they reached the foot of the spiral staircase. Anori gasped for breath and sputtered, "You took the icon, you mustn't steal! You nearly got us killed!"

Their hearts were hammering in their breasts. When they reached her chamber, Obsidiana turned to Anori and said: "I've never seen those people before! How come they know me?"

"You must know why! You are worshipped. These are the people who bring you sacrifices."

"Since when?"

"Since forever!" Anori said, exasperated. "Your soul dwells with the gods, but your body rests in the temple. Urchin the chaplain brings us messages from you. He says you are the only hope since the kingdom split into two and the king went to war."

"Who is this chaplain, Urchin? What gods? I don't understand!"

"You'll have to ask the king, he's on his way home."

"He's coming?" Obsidiana felt a flutter in her stomach.

"Yes, the queen announced it."

"The queen? What queen?"

"Queen Gunnhild, of course."

Obsidiana didn't know what to believe. "Gunnhild? Who's she?"

"Don't you know anything?"

"Why didn't you tell me about her?"

Anori was utterly perplexed. "You must know Queen Gunnhild."

Thoughts flew around Obsidiana's head, but she stood as if paralyzed.

"Quick, put the dress on," Anori said. "The monks will be coming for you any moment!"

Obsidiana stood still. "No, I'm not going back into the casket ever again! I need to see my father."

"But then they'll find me! They'll kill me. You have to get back in the casket, and I have to go!"

She saw the flash of fear in his eyes. Sighing, she cast off the cloak, put her dress on, and hurried to climb back into the casket. As she did so she banged her toe hard on a floorboard; she was almost in tears as Anori looked at her and said: "I'll be back!"

"Wait," she whispered, "don't shut it just yet. I need to think. I need time to think."

She closed her eyes and thought about the people in the square and about the butcher who was going to chop off her hand. And those unfamiliar names: Gunnhild, Urchin. What was going on? Heavy footsteps approached, and somebody slid aside the bolt on the door. Anori slammed the casket tightly shut and just managed to crawl out through the hole in the panel before the monks entered the chamber and carried the princess out onto the square. The people, who had barely recovered after the day's miracle, whispered: "Blood—there is blood in the casket!"

Blood

Time seeped into the casket. Obsidiana snatched her breath like a newborn lamb. Five black masks stared down at her.

"Look!" the voice behind the one of the masks said. "There's the drop of blood!" It was a female voice, one Obsidiana didn't recognize.

"The people in the square were terrified," the voice continued. "Look, another drop! What's happening? Is she dying? Can she go moldy in here? We were supposed to look after her!"

"I don't know," said a thoughtful male voice behind another mask. He was carrying a magnifying glass. Mopping sweat from his brow he added, "But her big toe is obviously bleeding."

"How could this happen? It should not be possible!" Obsidiana recognized Exel's voice. He addressed Obsidiana: "What happened? Did somebody hurt you? Why is your toe bleeding, princess? We'll throw the guards to the lions! I promise you that much!"

"I don't know. I guess I bashed my toe," she said.

"But that's fresh blood! It wasn't there yesterday. Obsidiana, tell us the truth. What happened? Has somebody been wasting your time?"

"May I ask you to stand up," the man with the magnifying glass said.

Obsidiana stood up. There was a bloody toe print on the floor. "Who are you? Where's my dad?"

The female voice screamed: "May the gods have mercy on us, the dress is covered with stains! And her feet are dirty! Where have you been? Heaven help us, I don't understand how this could happen!"

A man stood uneasily in the corner holding an hourglass; he trembled like a twig. "Somebody has been stealing time from her!"

The masked figures gasped. Obsidiana looked at them and at the man with the hourglass. She was scared: if they found the hole, bloodhounds would be able to follow the trail back to Anori's place.

"What day is it today?" Obsidiana asked. "Why can't I see your faces? Where is my dad?"

"The king will be here soon," replied an unfamiliar male voice.

"Are you Zee Urchin?" she asked. The others gasped.

"She recognizes you through the mask!" the female voice said.

"And are you Gunnhild?"

In a trembling voice, Urchin said: "I told you. She sees everything! She knows what we think."

"This is not real time, Obsidiana," the female voice said nervously. "The king is still away. You're not supposed to see us. We're not here! This is in-between time."

"The blood is a symbol," Urchin said. "It is a harbinger of great change. I have felt it for a long time."

Obsidiana took a deep breath. "What day is it? Where's my dad?" she repeated.

"Tell us what happened," said Gunnhild. "We're in a hurry; we may not waste your time on such trivialities."

"The casket opened accidentally. Suddenly it was just open. I wanted to let someone know, but the door was bolted. I wandered around the room in the dark and must have knocked my toe."

They removed a splinter from her toe, washed her feet, and put her in a new dress. She lay down again and sighed with relief; nobody was looking for the hole in the wall.

The timekeeper cleared his throat: "Come on! Hurry, hurry. Time marches on!"

"Now smile," said the female voice behind the mask. But Obsidiana couldn't smile. She tried to place the voice. Where did this woman come from?

"Where's my dad?"

"He'll be here any minute," said the female voice. "Now smile."

The lid snapped shut. When Obsidiana was carried out onto the city square, she looked a little sad—but not for long, because the next moment her father's beaming face greeted her.

The Opening Ceremony

"Papa!" she shouted. "You're back!"

Obsidiana leaped into her father's arms. She gazed at his face; he looked gaunt and drawn and was now more like the pictures of his grandfather than how she remembered him. His beard had become grizzled and shaggy.

"What happened to you?" she asked.

Dimon smiled. "It's just time, playing tricks on me," he said. He was missing some teeth and had lost a lot of hair. He looked at his daughter in disbelief; she hadn't changed a bit since he had left her. "I've missed you so much!" he said.

"You said you'd only be away for a year."

He shook his head. "I'm sorry, the world has been making life difficult for us. But today we are not going to worry about anything. We are going to throw a party in your honor."

"Is it my birthday?"

"No, today we're having an opening ceremony. The people want to see you, so we're going to celebrate. We must keep our spirits up. Let's go!" he said merrily.

Obsidiana almost had to run to keep up with him, as did the black-clad man with the hourglass. It was as if everything in the palace was moving at double speed. They sped along the corridors with servants running past, and the king talked as if he was in a race against time: "Come on now. There's no time to lose! The party is about to begin."

Flocks of crows perched on the windowsills. The king swept past issuing orders to his minions, who scribbled commands on bits of paper for the crows to fly off with.

"I have to introduce you to some new people in our lives," the king said. "I hope you will welcome them."

Obsidiana's ears pricked up.

"I have met a good woman called Gunnhild, and she has moved into the palace to live with us."

"Oh really?" *At last he mentions it*, she thought, not knowing whether this made her happy or mad.

"And you now have two sisters!"

"Two sisters?"

"Yes, this is going to be such a wonderful day for you." King Dimon led her down the stairs. The castle was spick-and-span and so brightly lit that not a single corner was in shadow. The staff lined the corridors to salute Obsidiana; every face bore an expression of fearful adulation, and many of them were in tears. Obsidiana had difficulty recognizing them. Guards she remembered were now somewhat larger than before, more wrinkled, and with furry, owl-like eyebrows; young ladies-in-waiting had grown older and stouter. Cooks and footmen, guards and officials bowed—and there was Thordis! She had changed so much that Obsidiana hardly knew her; the once black hair was now gathered in a long, white braid. Obsidiana flew toward her, but a guard stepped forward and caught her. Thordis took a step back and gave a formal curtsy.

"Nursie! Don't you recognize me? I'm back!" Obsidiana slipped from the guard's grasp and hugged Thordis, who responded firmly to the embrace, whispering sadly in her ear:

"My darling child! If only I had known it would come to this."

The black-clad timekeeper signaled, and the king barked, impatiently, "Hurry up! Every minute counts." A guard led Thordis away and others hurried Obsidiana along to the hall of mirrors, where attendants swathed her in golden silk. Then the king led her down a long corridor to where a tall lady was waiting for them; standing by her were two girls with enormous eyes and eyelashes so long that they looked like black butterflies on white flowers when the girls blinked. The lady curtsied and said: "It is a true honor for me to share some time with you, Obsidiana. My name is Gunnhild."

Her voice was soft as if she'd swallowed a mouthful of flour, but there was something strange about her smile, or rather her unsmiling eyes.

"Good day," Obsidiana replied. She looked toward her father and, though she felt as if her insides were exploding, smiled too. Thordis and Jako had taught her good manners.

Gunnhild glanced at the girls either side of her. Curtsying low, they said in unison: "Good day, dear sister."

Obsidiana stared at them. She had expected babies, but her sisters were taller than she was. They were very beautiful young women with neat little noses, deep dimples and black eyebrows. The sisters met her gaze with quizzical looks.

"But they are so old!" Obsidiana blurted. They frowned and one of them began to cry.

"There is no need to be rude," the new queen said kindly. "Not everybody is allowed to step aside from time like you do!"

Obsidiana was sure that this was all a dream—as if her dreams had settled in her head like leaves on the bottom of a pond. The casket must have opened into another world where everything happened too quickly. *How many years have passed?* she wondered. *Maybe four? Ten?* But the sisters seemed much older than that.

The doors of the ceremonial hall swung open and a fanfare sounded. Under glittering gold chandeliers, the chieftains of

Pangea's various tribes came to meet her, clad in a dazzling mixture of national costumes. They offered gifts—cloaks made of peacock feathers, diamond chains, rubies and emeralds, zeolites, exquisite sausages, caviar and fruits, and hundred-year-old fine wines from countries with easy names such as Po or Xi or long incomprehensible strings of sounds that she didn't understand.

Obsidiana looked at all these smartly dressed people and saw how they whispered and stared at her. Nobody had seen her walk, move, or talk for many years.

She sat shyly down at the table and finally managed to ask her father: "When were my sisters born?"

Before her father could reply, the timekeeper rang a bell. The king motioned to Consiglio, who stood up and gave a crisp hand signal, at which the hall fell quiet so suddenly that it was as if the silence had been rehearsed. She hardly recognized Consiglio; the bees that always accompanied him seemed weary and sat on his head like yellow pimples.

The king rose to his feet and a murmur went around the hall.

"As you can see," he said, "time has not been kind to me; but worry not, Obsidiana will be with us forever, or as the poet put it:

> *Graceful as a swallow,*
> *guileless as a lamb,*
> *golden is her beauty—the whole world's charm."*

Dimon raised his arms, and drapes opened to reveal the palace gardens, where trapeze artists danced, fire-eaters and clowns performed, and minstrels played and sang. Obsidiana tried to make contact with her father—there were questions burning on her lips—but the king couldn't hear her over all the commotion.

He just smiled and pointed at other drapes that were suddenly drawn apart, and a herd of giraffes ran through the gardens—yellow with spots and with long, graceful necks. They were like nothing she had ever seen before.

Her father laughed, and Gunnhild seemed proud. Obsidiana rubbed her eyes and studied her sisters; they were tall and beautiful and wore elegant dresses, and yet they looked vacant. A door opened, and a man entered wearing a strange hat and a golden robe embroidered with two closed eyes. The outfit was so absurd that she almost burst out laughing, but then she saw his expression; he was obviously not a court jester. The man approached her, kissed her hand and said, loud enough for all to hear:

"My name is Zee Urchin! I'm very pleased to meet you. I have observed you in your casket but never had the opportunity to touch you." He began assiduously to stroke her hand; she tried to draw it back, but Urchin held tightly onto it. He raised it above her head and addressed the assembly: "I bring you the blessing of the Eternal Princess! Pangea has endured many trials over the last twenty years, but thanks to the princess the dynasty will reign forever. If you follow her guidance, she can ensure the gods' eternal approval. She is the Falcon of Paradise, she is the Albino Flower. She has power over the seasons and over days and nights. Though she was born more than thirty-five years ago, she is still fourteen. She is living proof that even time has to bow to the might of King Dimon!"

Gunnhild smiled and clapped happily, as did the princesses. The assembly cheered. Gunnhild nudged Obsidiana, who curtsied. She couldn't believe her own ears. Had she been in the casket for twenty years? Was she thirty-five? She looked at her father. Yes, he could easily be twenty years older than he had been the last time she saw him.

"You misunderstand," Obsidiana whispered to her father. "I wasn't with the gods!"

A group of monks walked briskly toward her with strange, dance-like steps. Their leader took her hand and conducted her through the castle to the balcony overlooking the square. A swirling mass of people surged forward in front of the castle, shouting, "LONG LIVE PRINCESS OBSIDIANA!" She gazed in amazement at the immense throng of flag-waving people; she had never seen anything like it. Scanning the crowd, she at last spotted a boy standing on a tall pillar and waving an orange flag. *That looks like Anori*, she thought, so she gave her very best smile and waved. The mob went crazy and the cheering became even louder. She who had seemed to be asleep for all these years was suddenly standing in front of her people, looking very much alive.

A bell rang out in the temple. A million swallows appeared like a cloud in the sky, turning and swerving to form letters and flowers as Consiglio conducted them like a bandmaster. Obsidiana, wide-eyed with surprise, burst into a peal of laughter. They turned back to the banqueting hall, where a thousand footmen served the finest gourmet dishes.

Every tiniest fraction of a second had been planned to the smallest detail. At regular intervals the timekeeper struck a bell, and it felt as if the rhythm he was beating became faster and faster so that the banquet proceeded ever more rapidly. People ate, laughed, and moved in rhythm, but at a tempo that suggested that the entire feast had been carefully rehearsed. *How can they laugh so fast?* Obsidiana wondered.

All sorrow was to be forgotten now. Music sounded to signal the start of a grand ball, and soon young gentlemen were sweeping Obsidiana around the dance floor, so that the evening spun around her like a Ferris wheel and she forgot all about time. She was momentarily distracted by the sight of her father standing in a side room with a group of important-looking men, one of whom was waving his hands about, obviously agitated. She was beginning to wonder whether this meant bad news, when someone took her hand.

"My name is Orri, son of the Duke of Plains. May I have the honor of this dance?" She looked into his beautiful blue-gray eyes and was soon rapturously whirling across the floor with him—round and round. Catching sight of the duke and the king watching them approvingly, she blushed a little and allowed Orri to take her on another turn around the dance floor. She would have liked to stop and talk with him, but the timekeeper rang the bell; Orri kissed her hand and took leave of her. Maids clad in white appeared and escorted her to a bedchamber, where they led her to a bed made up with silk coverlets; she lay down and looked up at the ceiling, a smile on her lips. Her father came in to say goodnight. The man with the hourglass came too.

"What a happy day this has been," Obsidiana said. "I'm glad you've come back."

With an eye on the sand sifting through the hourglass, the king got straight to the point.

"You're tired after a long day, my darling. I'm afraid you'll have to sleep tonight; I believe there isn't any sleep in the casket."

He tucked the comforter around her, but she asked anxiously: "Why did you let me miss twenty years?"

Dimon stared distantly into space. "You didn't miss anything in those years. They were not good for us. All your days should be happy days."

"But one can cry even when the sun shines outside," she said, "and laugh when it's raining and windy. You never told me about Gunnhild and my sisters."

"The time was never right. We wanted to do it properly. It has taken Gunnhild two years to organize this day. She wanted you to enjoy it. This is how all your days should be, dear daughter, and this is how they all can be."

"Surely not tomorrow as well?"

"No—tomorrow will be spent cleaning up the palace, and the people will be waiting for you at the temple. You will be with the gods tomorrow."

At the temple? she thought. "No!" She cried. "Not yet! Not yet!"

"Representatives from the Cloud Mountains came to see me yesterday. There is a state of emergency there and they are expecting me tomorrow. Our future is at stake."

"No! Don't go yet! What will happen to me?"

"Before you know it we will spend another lovely day together. Don't worry about time. It's only mortals who suffer from it."

Obsidiana shook her head. "I don't want to go to the square," she whispered. She sat up and stared at her father. She looked at his hands and hair, his deep wrinkles and tired eyes. She found it difficult to match him with her most recent memories.

The king was about to reply when the timekeeper cleared his throat. "Your Majesty! Time marches on!"

"If I'm always in the casket you will go a long time before me," Obsidiana said.

"What do you mean?"

"I'll still be young when you die."

The king sighed. "The whole world loves you and will do so forever, whereas most people are only loved by a few for a short while."

"But Jako said it was better to be loved by one person whom you love in return than being worshipped by millions you don't know! What's the value of love that isn't mutual?"

133

"You will meet people who will be born a hundred years hence and still another thousand years hence. It's painful to be always saying goodbye, but it's worse to watch your time being eaten away and disappearing into the void. There are exciting times ahead for you."

Obsidiana was finding it difficult to breathe. "But why? Why does the kingdom have to be so big?"

"Royal dynasties that are overthrown suffer a cruel fate, dear daughter. That's how it is. It's a cruel world."

"But you're the king of the whole world! You can stop the cruelty!"

Dimon wiped a tear from her eye. "I'm fighting for a better world. That I can promise."

"I want to say goodnight to Thordis."

"Thordis?" said the king, his thoughts elsewhere. "Yes, it can probably be arranged if that's what you wish. But not for long!" He stroked her head and tucked the blankets around her. *Be careful in the war*, Obsidiana thought as he left; but she didn't say it—the lump in her throat was so big she couldn't speak.

Obsidiana lay awake in her bed. The day seemed like a bubbling broth in her head. She smiled to herself as she thought about the ball and all the sons of noblemen; she had never danced so much in one evening. But then it all seemed overwhelming—how long would she have to be in the casket this time?

She heard light footsteps outside. Thordis appeared in the doorway and tiptoed over to her. She stroked Obsidiana gently and kissed her forehead.

"I've tried everything, my darling child." A tear glistened in her eye as Obsidiana embraced her. "I remember the first time I took you in my arms. I remember when you began to walk and speak.

You were such a funny child when you and the panda were running around the palace. Now suddenly all those years have passed!"

"Please can you make sure I don't stay long in the casket?"

Thordis heaved a heavy sigh.

"Even though I breastfed you, you're not mine. I have no power any more, my little wishy. You're a goddess. You are worshipped. The king couldn't let you out even if he wanted to," she whispered.

"What do you mean?"

"You are keeping the state afloat. The sacrifices pay for the country's defenses. The city depends on the offerings that all your worshippers bring, and if you weren't in the square every day the kingdom would have long since collapsed. Exel's calculations prove it."

The timekeeper now came in and said sharply: "She is to go to sleep at once. I have strict instructions!"

"Be sure to take good care of yourself," said Thordis, kissing the top of her head. "I don't know how much longer I will be with you."

And so Obsidiana fell asleep. Now it was as though a dam burst, and twenty years of dreams surged through her head like a tsunami. She saw Anori growing taller and taller like a sprouting bean. She danced with dwarfs and giraffes until suddenly she was swimming, and then the water turned to sand and she got sucked down by a whirlpool in an hourglass. She fell into a forest hollow where her mother sat sad-faced, opened her eyes wide and said: "Be careful!"

Obsidiana tried to reach out to her but felt herself breaking out in a cold sweat. She didn't want to wake up, but when she opened her eyes she saw Gunnhild standing there, lips pursed. Obsidiana gave a start and snuggled beneath her comforter. When she plucked up the courage to take another peek, her stepmother was gone.

Day and Night

Obsidiana was afraid to go back to sleep. And she needed to think. The dawn chorus was just beginning, but the palace would not wake for several hours. She lit a lamp. She was haunted by that number—twenty years! She took down her diaries from their bookshelf. There were thirty-five of them, but only fifteen were familiar to her; twenty were entirely blank, page after empty page. She did the math:

"365 days in each year. That means 3,650 days in ten years, and in twenty years . . . 7,300 days."

She tried to imagine 7,300 days. She closed her eyes and said out loud, as slowly as she could:

"Sun rises. Day. Sun crosses the heavens. Sun sets. Night." She picked up a diary, found the first day she had missed, and wrote Day. Then she wrote Night; then Day and Night again and again, scribbling faster and faster Day Night Day Night and then in capital letters:

DAY NIGHT DAY NIGHT DAY NIGHT DAY NIGHT DAY NIGHT DAY NIGHT
DAY NIGHT DAY NIGHT DAY NIGHT DAY NIGHT DAY NIGHT DAY NIGHT
DAY NIGHT DAY NIGHT DAY NIGHT DAY NIGHT DAY NIGHT DAY NIGHT
DAY NIGHT DAY NIGHT DAY NIGHT DAY NIGHT DAY NIGHT DAY NIGHT
DAY NIGHT DAY NIGHT DAY NIGHT DAY NIGHT DAY NIGHT DAY NIGHT
DAY NIGHT DAY NIGHT DAY NIGHT DAY NIGHT DAY NIGHT DAY NIGHT
DAY NIGHT DAY NIGHT DAY NIGHT DAY NIGHT DAY NIGHT DAY NIGHT

136

DAY NIGHT DAY NIGHT DAY NIGHT DAY NIGHT DAY NIGHT DAY NIGHT
DAY NIGHT DAY NIGHT DAY NIGHT DAY NIGHT DAY NIGHT DAY NIGHT
DAY NIGHT DAY NIGHT DAY NIGHT DAY NIGHT DAY NIGHT DAY NIGHT
DAY NIGHT DAY NIGHT DAY NIGHT DAY NIGHT DAY NIGHT DAY NIGHT
DAY NIGHT DAY NIGHT DAY NIGHT DAY NIGHT DAY NIGHT DAY NIGHT
DAY NIGHT DAY NIGHT DAY NIGHT DAY NIGHT DAY NIGHT DAY NIGHT
DAY NIGHT DAY NIGHT DAY NIGHT DAY NIGHT DAY NIGHT DAY NIGHT
DAY NIGHT DAY NIGHT DAY NIGHT DAY NIGHT DAY NIGHT DAY NIGHT
DAY NIGHT DAY NIGHT DAY NIGHT DAY NIGHT DAY NIGHT DAY NIGHT
DAY NIGHT DAY NIGHT DAY NIGHT DAY NIGHT DAY NIGHT DAY NIGHT
DAY NIGHT DAY NIGHT DAY NIGHT DAY NIGHT DAY NIGHT DAY NIGHT
DAY NIGHT DAY NIGHT DAY NIGHT DAY NIGHT DAY NIGHT DAY NIGHT
DAY NIGHT DAY NIGHT DAY NIGHT DAY NIGHT DAY NIGHT DAY NIGHT
DAY NIGHT DAY NIGHT DAY NIGHT DAY NIGHT DAY NIGHT DAY NIGHT
DAY NIGHT DAY NIGHT DAY NIGHT DAY NIGHT DAY NIGHT DAY NIGHT
DAY NIGHT DAY NIGHT DAY NIGHT DAY NIGHT DAY NIGHT DAY NIGHT
DAY NIGHT DAY NIGHT DAY NIGHT DAY NIGHT DAY NIGHT DAY NIGHT
DAY NIGHT DAY NIGHT DAY NIGHT DAY NIGHT DAY NIGHT DAY NIGHT
DAY NIGHT DAY NIGHT DAY NIGHT DAY NIGHT DAY NIGHT DAY NIGHT
DAY NIGHT DAY NIGHT DAY NIGHT DAY NIGHT DAY NIGHT DAY NIGHT
DAY NIGHT DAY NIGHT DAY NIGHT DAY NIGHT DAY NIGHT DAY NIGHT
DAY NIGHT DAY NIGHT DAY NIGHT DAY NIGHT DAY NIGHT DAY NIGHT
DAY NIGHT DAY NIGHT DAY NIGHT DAY NIGHT DAY NIGHT DAY NIGHT
DAY NIGHT DAY NIGHT DAY NIGHT DAY NIGHT DAY NIGHT DAY NIGHT
DAY NIGHT DAY NIGHT DAY NIGHT DAY NIGHT DAY NIGHT DAY NIGHT
DAY NIGHT DAY NIGHT DAY NIGHT DAY NIGHT DAY NIGHT DAY NIGHT
DAY NIGHT DAY NIGHT DAY NIGHT DAY NIGHT DAY NIGHT DAY NIGHT
DAY NIGHT DAY NIGHT DAY NIGHT DAY NIGHT DAY NIGHT DAY NIGHT
DAY NIGHT DAY NIGHT DAY NIGHT DAY NIGHT DAY NIGHT DAY NIGHT
DAY NIGHT DAY NIGHT DAY NIGHT DAY NIGHT DAY NIGHT DAY NIGHT
DAY NIGHT DAY NIGHT DAY NIGHT DAY NIGHT DAY NIGHT DAY NIGHT

DAY NIGHT DAY NIGHT DAY NIGHT DAY NIGHT DAY NIGHT DAY NIGHT
DAY NIGHT DAY NIGHT DAY NIGHT DAY NIGHT DAY NIGHT DAY NIGHT
DAY NIGHT DAY NIGHT DAY NIGHT DAY NIGHT DAY NIGHT DAY NIGHT
DAY NIGHT DAY NIGHT DAY NIGHT DAY NIGHT DAY NIGHT DAY NIGHT
DAY NIGHT DAY NIGHT DAY NIGHT DAY NIGHT DAY NIGHT DAY NIGHT
DAY NIGHT DAY NIGHT DAY NIGHT DAY NIGHT DAY NIGHT DAY NIGHT
DAY NIGHT DAY NIGHT DAY NIGHT DAY NIGHT DAY NIGHT DAY NIGHT
DAY NIGHT DAY NIGHT DAY NIGHT DAY NIGHT DAY NIGHT DAY NIGHT
DAY NIGHT DAY NIGHT DAY NIGHT DAY NIGHT DAY NIGHT DAY NIGHT
DAY NIGHT DAY NIGHT DAY NIGHT DAY NIGHT DAY NIGHT DAY NIGHT
DAY NIGHT DAY NIGHT DAY NIGHT DAY NIGHT DAY NIGHT DAY NIGHT
DAY NIGHT DAY NIGHT DAY NIGHT DAY NIGHT DAY NIGHT DAY NIGHT
DAY NIGHT DAY NIGHT DAY NIGHT DAY NIGHT DAY NIGHT DAY NIGHT
DAY NIGHT DAY NIGHT DAY NIGHT DAY NIGHT DAY NIGHT DAY NIGHT
DAY NIGHT DAY NIGHT DAY NIGHT DAY NIGHT DAY NIGHT DAY NIGHT
DAY NIGHT DAY NIGHT DAY NIGHT DAY NIGHT DAY NIGHT DAY NIGHT
DAY NIGHT DAY NIGHT DAY NIGHT DAY NIGHT DAY NIGHT DAY NIGHT
DAY NIGHT DAY NIGHT DAY NIGHT DAY NIGHT DAY NIGHT DAY NIGHT
DAY NIGHT DAY NIGHT DAY NIGHT DAY NIGHT DAY NIGHT DAY NIGHT
DAY NIGHT DAY NIGHT DAY NIGHT DAY NIGHT DAY NIGHT DAY NIGHT
DAY NIGHT DAY NIGHT DAY NIGHT DAY NIGHT DAY NIGHT

By now her wrist was hurting. She paged through the book, counting. 365 days. 365 nights. That's what one year looked like. She had lost more than twenty of them. Every pair of words represented a whole day that contained hours and minutes and moments; rain and wind, sun and clouds, rainbows and thunder, and cocoons that would become butterflies. She scribbled right across one page in enormous letters: DAY and on the next page: NIGHT.

Obsidiana was furious. How could they do this to her? How could they! She saw a cockroach scuttling across the floor and stamped on it, squashing it with her bare foot.

She thought about Peak and Moon. She wondered what the lifespan of deer was. She opened the door, went out into the corridor, and started running through the darkness of the palace, emerging finally into the palace gardens. She looked around. Nothing but an outline remained of the pond, now dried up with weeds growing on the bottom. There were no huge goldfish anymore and her little rhinoceros and elephant were nowhere to be seen.

"Oh no!" she whispered. The little forest was parched; just a few withered trunks. "Peak! Moon!" she whispered, but they did not come to her. She fought back her tears. "Peak! Moon! Where are you?"

The door to Jako's room was open. Warily, she peeped inside, but instead of Jako's old chair all that met her gaze was a dusty storeroom; hanging on the wall was an old motto: EACH DAY IS AN UNPOLISHED DIAMOND.

She was heartbroken. *Was Jako gone?* Obsidiana needed to talk to her father.

The guests had all left, but the aromas left behind from the feast still hung in the air. She searched through halls and antechambers until at last she caught sight of him in his office. She stopped in the doorway and looked inside. The king was pacing the floor, crimson-faced. Exel and Consiglio were also in the room, along with some military officers she didn't know, and two men she recognized from the banquet, dressed in peculiar national costumes.

"NO? What does no mean? It's an outrage!" the king said.

"Your Majesty," said one of the two men, "the people have stopped obeying us. They don't send sacrifices when they have no food!"

"We'll go immediately," Dimon growled. "We'll teach them a lesson."

His eyes flashed with anger and his fists were clenched, white-knuckled.

"Be merciful, Sire. There are women and children there."

"There will be no mercy for those who hide behind women and children!"

"I object, your Majesty," the other man said.

"Guards, seize him!" the king yelled. "Throw him to the lions!"

Obsidiana crept aside and tried to hide behind a marble column. The guards escorted the man out into the corridor, and Obsidiana held her breath as they passed, but the man saw her and threw himself at her feet.

"Why are you so cruel? What have I done to you? Have mercy on me, Eternal Princess!"

The guards also seemed to fear her but did not dare address her; they stood transfixed and stared at her as if she were a ghost.

"I was just looking for a glass of water," she whispered. "I was thirsty."

She ran off. Her father was fighting for a better world, but why did he have to be so angry? Was he really going to throw the man to the lions?

The palace was still in darkness. On their windowsill roosts, the crows cawed and fidgeted their wings. She had almost retraced her steps back to the bedchamber when she heard voices in the corridor and stopped to listen; it was Gunnhild and Urchin.

Gunnhild sounded downcast: "Why doesn't she like me?"

"The Eternal Princess says that you have to do better. You must take care with your thoughts."

"But I've tried to send her good thoughts."

Urchin whispered: "She knows that you envy her. The Eternal Princess knows that you hate her."

"I don't hate her, I just don't understand why she never wanted to meet my little girls."

"You know they are mortal," said Urchin. "If Obsidiana bonds with mortals her days will be filled with sorrow and heartache when everything grows away from her. You may eat breakfast with her. But the gods need her. It is vital she goes back into the casket as soon as possible!"

Obsidiana froze. Were they all losing their minds? She heard horses being harnessed outside and ran to the window. Torches flickered in the castle forecourt; the king and his entourage were all set to go. *No!* she thought. *He mustn't go!* She shouted as loud as she could, her voice all but drowned by the trumpet flourishes:

"Wait, Papa! Don't go yet! I need to tell you—!"

The king looked back.

"I'll return in no time at all!"

The company rode out of the city into the darkness. Gradually the sound of trumpets and hoofbeats faded, and in no time King Dimon had disappeared beyond mountains and marshes, over lands and oceans, way beyond the horizon. Obsidiana slipped back into bed. It took her a long time to fall asleep, and when at last she closed her eyes she could see nothing but endless lists of words flying past: NIGHT! DAY!

Sisters

Obsidiana was woken by four maids, one carrying a comb, another a dress, the third a cardigan, and the fourth an emerald-green crown. They approached her in formation—every movement so orderly and detached.

"Where is my nursemaid?" she asked. But the women did not reply. "Where is Thordis?" she asked again. They took a step back and looked at their feet. "Why won't you answer me?" The maids looked away. There was the sound of footsteps, and then Gunnhild entered the room.

"I came to see you last night," she said. "You were calling for your mother."

"Yes, she came to me in a dream."

"You're just like your father; on the rare occasions he sleeps, he calls for her too."

"Where is my nurse?"

"She works in the kitchen now."

"I have to see her!"

"I'm afraid there's no time for that. We're about to eat breakfast."

They went into the dining hall, where the two princesses sat waiting. The staff bowed but avoided catching Obsidiana's eye.

The two girls seemed to have pincushions for tongues; they spat needles with every word.

"Do you remember when Papa gave us the little white deer?" said one of the sisters.

"Yes," said the other. "I miss Peak and Moon." Obsidiana felt a stab of pain in her stomach. Did they know Peak and Moon?

"Do you recall when Papa went hunting with us?"

"Was Dad not away at the war?" Obsidiana interrupted.

"No, not always."

"Why wasn't I allowed to go too?"

"Surely you're not jealous?" said the queen.

"No, but it might have been fun to go too."

"Now you're being ungrateful. You are worshipped and immortal and yet you want more!"

Obsidiana looked at the queen's hands as she spoke; her fingers were like crooked twigs. Gunnhild laid a hand on Obsidiana's shoulder and drummed her fingers as if to hurry her along. Obsidiana turned and caught sight of the pale timekeeper standing in a corner with his hourglass; she started so violently that she spilled milk everywhere. The queen called out: "Footmen! Quick, another glass! Don't hang about! She needs another glass! She needs to be at the temple by midday."

Obsidiana shook her head. "No, I'm not going back to the temple!"

The queen looked at her. "There were half a million people in the square yesterday! Many have been traveling for months on end. The kingdom needs you! Troops are waiting in the battlefield for supplies, which they won't get unless you are in your place at the temple. You can't just think about yourself."

"No, I don't want to," Obsidiana said. "I don't want to!" She looked for an escape route.

"You ungrateful child!" said the queen. She pulled a gray hair from her head and pointed at a gold tooth in her mouth. "Look at me, do you think I want to get older like a serving maid?

Don't you think I'd like my girls to have a casket too? The king said goodbye to you before he left, but did he say goodbye to us? No, he did not!"

Obsidiana looked at her. She felt sorry for this woman, who was so very angry; for one moment she felt hope, and said as gently as she could:

"The girls can have the casket! They can keep it!" But instead of softening the queen became furious.

"Do you think the people would accept that? My girls are not the Eternal Princess! Do you think that I never asked?"

The words became a buzz in Obsidiana's head. She closed her eyes and saw white stars floating behind her eyelids.

"Wasn't the opening feast fun?" said Gunnhild, in a somewhat calmer tone.

"Yes, it was."

"Wasn't it all for your benefit?"

"Yes."

"Do you think it's nice to behave like this toward someone who spent two years preparing the perfect day for you?" She gritted her teeth and spoke harshly. "Urchin told me exactly how you wanted your day to be."

Obsidiana, hoping to find a soft spot, put on her most appealing expression and asked: "Could I please have one more day? Just an ordinary one. You don't have to prepare anything."

Gunnhild reddened. "Oh, thank you," she said bitterly. "So it's all the same to you whether the day is two years in preparation or not! But what about the people out there? Do you want to keep millions waiting for you for just one ordinary day? Everything would go crazy! It would cost lives!"

Obsidiana thought of the casket. Yes, right now she would like to shut herself in it and make this conversation evaporate into thin air. Urchin had clearly told Gunnhild a load of non-sense.

"Have you thanked me for what I did for you?" The buzzing in Obsidiana's ears grew louder. "Have you even asked what your sisters' names are?"

"No," said Obsidiana quietly, feeling somewhat ashamed. "There was never any time, there was such a lot going on."

"You are so self-centered. Their names are Silverwillow and Goldwillow. Your father has sacrificed everything for you. He is wrestling with the earth itself, which split into two all because of you!"

"Because of me? What do you mean?"

"All of this is because of you, and now you want to keep millions of people waiting just so you can have an ordinary day!"

Gunnhild stormed out, slamming the door behind her. Seven monks approached to escort Obsidiana to the casket. She tried to run away, but they were quick to corner her. She stamped her feet and hissed at them.

"NO! I will not go into the casket!" she screamed. She scratched one of them, drawing blood, and he murmured: "Thank you, my dear, thank you," as if he was actually grateful.

They grasped her by her arms and legs and lifted her up into the casket. She fought back and put on an ugly frown as they closed the lid; she looked just like a witch. Somebody instantly re-opened the casket and she saw that Gunnhild was almost in tears.

"Will you please try and behave properly! You are ungrateful and spoiled!"

Obsidiana tried to sit up but her stepmother pushed her back, digging her nails into her chest. As the lid of the casket slammed down Obsidiana was looking daggers at the queen.

And so her face was stuck in a terrible frown. Her stepmother looked at her haughtily and said: "At last the people get to see you as you really are. Urchin! Monks! Carry the witch out onto the square!"

Frozen Time

Grace took a break from reading and disappeared into the kitchen to make herself some coffee. Peter sat silently in a corner. How had he ended up here, in an old woman's house in the middle of a ghost town?

It had been a regular Saturday when Peter's doorbell rang, and he answered it to find a man standing on the step, wearing a pin-striped suit and sunglasses, and with hair so gelled down that it wouldn't have tousled in a hurricane.

"Your mom in?"

Peter called for his mom. The man with the unnaturally smooth hair drew out a black-and-white photograph of a guy with a crew cut and a rather dumb expression. "Have you seen this man before?"

"No, sorry," Peter's mother replied. She tried to close the door, but the man blocked it with his foot.

"Pardon me, dear madam, but I haven't told you the whole story. I'm carrying out a survey for TimeBox®."

She opened wider and the man showed her the picture again. "This is Igor the Terrible. He was a famous thief and mass murderer in Russia."

"Good heavens! That's shocking."

Peter stood apart and listened; his friend Skyler had come by and was playing with his cell phone.

"This loathsome man robbed poor widows of their money and made minced meat and sausages out of his victims."

She took a closer look at the picture. "I find that hard to believe," she said. "He doesn't seem the type to know how to make sausages."

"The bottom line is that he got twenty-five years in jail," said the man.

Overhearing the conversation, Skyler googled "Igor the Terrible" and "sausages" but couldn't find anything. He showed Peter the results.

"Mom, Igor the Terrible never existed," whispered Peter.

Somewhat embarrassed, the man replied: "Well, he wasn't exactly a murderer, but he worked in a bank and bankrupted many families."

"How did he do that?"

"He bought himself a sharp suit and created a website called higherinterest.com. Thousands of people deposited their life savings with him before he absconded with the money. The judge handed down a twenty-five-year sentence."

"What a dreadful man! Is this true, Peter?"

Skyler looked it up on his phone. "Yes, it's true, except he didn't get the prison sentence." Now the man in the suit became really rattled; these boys were upsetting his line of argument.

"But now I have to ask you just one question on behalf of TimeBox®." He fished out a file and brandished his pen in preparation for ticking the appropriate box. "WHAT MAKES YOU NO BETTER THAN A BANK ROBBER AND CANNIBAL?"

"What on earth do you mean?" said Peter's mom in astonishment.

The salesman was clearly well practiced in the art of shocking people and had now gotten into his stride.

"This is bullshit!" she exclaimed, and made as if to slam the door in his face.

"The bottom line is that you are a prisoner! You are a prisoner of time!"

The conversation was getting completely ridiculous. "I'm sorry, mister, but I'm a busy woman and have no time for evangelizers."

"You are a prisoner of time! The weather forecast is, for instance, pretty grim all week. And what are you going to do if it rains for the rest of the summer? Nothing? You'll just serve your sentence! The rainy summer will be your prison. Your sentence!"

"Right. I've had enough now," Peter's mother said.

"Just imagine," he said, raising his voice and upping the persuasion quotient, "Mondays are one seventh of your life; February and November occupy a sixth of it; and long, dark winter days fill a quarter of it. At the end of your life you'll think: Oh my God, did I spend thirty years in rain and mizzle? Oh, Days! Oh, Life! Where did you go?"

At this point a jaunty jingle sounded, the door of a delivery van standing at the curb opened, and two guys climbed out with a black casket the size of a slim refrigerator.

"Anything that goes into this box is protected from time. You can look at the weather forecast Monday and if you don't like it you can set the casket like an alarm clock and say: Adios amigos! See you Thursday!"

Peter's dad got up from his computer and came to the door. The salesman looked more than ever like a magician as he stood there spinning the casket round and round; all he needed to complete the picture was a saw, a cloak, and a top hat.

"Not long now until November," the man said, faking a shudder. "It's not really snowing yet but the fall leaves have dropped; it's cold but not cold enough to go skiing. With this casket, you could forget November, that damp, gray month, it'll flash by in an instant. Or you could go on a romantic trip abroad next week without having to worry about a babysitter for this little piggy," he said, pointing at Peter.

The man offered a contract and a pen. Peter's dad looked at his wife, who stared dreamily at him. He signed the contract.

The TimeBox® became an integral part of the family's daily life; soon there were three of them. But nothing worthy of note happened until Skyler's tenth birthday party approached. Peter was a particularly impatient child and asked continually: "Is it his birthday today? Is it his birthday today?" He had put on his party clothes and wrapped the Lego set he was planning to give his friend, and asked repeatedly: "Is it his birthday now?" His mom needed to pop out to the store and she had no time for a pestering child, so she shoved him into the box while she went. A moment later, or so it seemed to him, the box opened again, and he rushed off without looking back. His mom yelled after him: "Peter! Peter! Wait!"

But he ran off down the road clutching the birthday gift without listening to his mother. It was high summer and the trees were in leaf, but it wasn't until he got to Skyler's house that he realized something had changed. Last he remembered, the house had been white, but now it was red. He wondered if he'd maybe entered the wrong yard, but then he spotted Skyler's name on the doorbell.

Peter pushed the button. A tall figure answered the door. Peter gazed upward.

"Is Skyler in?"

"Yes, that's me," a deep male voice replied. He was over six feet tall with the beginnings of a beard.

"No, I'm looking for Skyler Fredericks," said Peter.

"Yes, that's me. I'm Skyler Fredericks." He bent down to take a closer look at the boy. "Is that you, Peter?"

"Yes," said Peter in a small voice, handing him the package.

"Wow, thanks. Would you like to come on in?"

Peter kicked off his shoes and strode confidently into Skyler's room as he was used to, but backed off when he saw a girl sitting on the bed reading a fashion magazine. He ran into the kitchen.

"It's seven years since I invited you to my birthday party," Skyler said.

"What? What d'you mean?"

"You're late, Peter. You forgot to look at the calendar. It's not my birthday today. And it's not even January!"

"Yes, I'm sorry I'm so late. Mom went out shopping. Something must have happened."

"I waited for you," said Skyler, unwrapping the gift. "I called by your house, but your mom said she was off to India to try to find herself. When she came back your dad had lost himself and gone to work in Finland. I often called by to ask about you. I missed you—I mean, we were best friends."

Peter was at a loss for words. They sat facing each other, silent. Skyler gave Peter a glass of milk.

Skyler examined his gift, a magnificent box of Lego. "Are you still collecting Star Wars Lego?" Peter asked. "We could put it together now?"

Skyler's face took on a slightly embarrassed look. "Peter, you're lost in time. It'll take you a little while to orient yourself, and I have homework I need to do."

"Homework?"

"Yes, I've got a physics exam tomorrow. I finish high school next year."

151

He paused. "We've obviously grown apart," he added.

"Yes, it looks like it." Suddenly Peter had an idea. "How about you waiting this time, Sky? If you wait for me, then we can be the same age again!"

"I don't know, Peter, I mean, I have a girlfriend."

Peter giggled and chanted: "HA! HA! Skyler has a girlfriend! Skyler has a girlfriend!" But he quickly realized how childish he was being.

Skyler rattled the box of Lego. The girl entered and looked at it.

"This is Inga, my girlfriend."

"Cool retro gift," she said.

"Thanks anyway, Peter," Skyler said.

"Might see you Friday," Peter said.

Skyler looked at Inga. "We're going to the movies, but I'm afraid it's R-rated."

"Maybe we can babysit you some other time," said Inga cheerfully.

"Babysit me? I don't need babysitters!" Peter ran back home feeling hurt and angry. He was met by his mom and kicked off his shoes and threw his jacket on the floor.

"Friends come and go, Peter dear," said his mother. "Sometimes friends grow apart. Aren't you glad you've still got your teenage years to look forward to while Skyler does nothing but hang out with his girlfriend? Go out and play. There are lots of kids here who can be your friends."

Peter said nothing. He went off to play in the local schoolyard. There were a few kids there, but he didn't recognize any faces except for one boy who had been at nursery school last time he remembered but now was clearly older than him. Peter went straight back home.

"Is Dad in Finland?" he asked.

152

"No, he's at the hardware store buying paint."

"Tell him to come home now!" Peter said angrily.

"He won't be back until the evening."

"I want to talk to him right now! NOW!" She shook her head tiredly. *Is he always going to be so impatient?* she thought. She opened one of the caskets.

"Okay, use the casket if you don't want to wait!"

Peter jumped into the box. Next thing he knew, an unfamiliar girl in a blue coat stood before him.

"Hi, I'm Kristin," she said. "You must come with me. Hurry!"

Peter followed her through an abandoned town to a house where an elderly woman and a group of children seemed to be living. Peter looked at the skull lying on the living-room table and couldn't fathom what was going on at all.

Grace walked around with her cup of coffee and pointed at the TimeBox® sign showing on the screen on the wall.

"Most of you vanished into caskets during the early years of TimeBox's operations. The company grew at an astonishing rate and within a short time its black boxes were everywhere. It became something of a craze. There were flashing signs all over with messages like: 'RAIN TOMORROW! TimeBox®!' The streets became empty on rainy days, and people forgot the words for stormy, sleet, or slush. Airplanes were modified so that time stopped in the passenger cabin as soon as the doors were closed, and to the passengers a flight across the Atlantic Ocean seemed to last no more than a second. Then the financial crisis struck, and the economists predicted a terrible year. 'DON'T LET THE CRISIS RUIN YOUR LIFE! TimeBox®!' Parents were advised to protect their children from these dreadful times, and that meant teachers lost their jobs so that they, too, disappeared into their own caskets. With fewer customers around, stores lost business and the sales staff bought caskets. All this caused a reduction in tax revenue, which led to cutbacks in the state health service, so sick people on waiting lists were placed into caskets, which meant that doctors got caskets for themselves. Now there was nobody to eat all the food that farmers were producing, so they put their livestock into caskets and asked the government what it planned to do."

"What did it do?"

"They got caskets and shut themselves away too."

"Did everybody disappear, then?"

"Every city had a few oddballs who decided to sit it out, but life was lonesome for them, and one after another they gradually disappeared into caskets until I was the only one left."

"How long ago did this happen?"

"I don't know. I don't keep track of time."

"This is dreadful."

"Yes, it was dreadful at first, but then the animals came, and the world seemed to get better and better. Each year more migrating birds arrived. The streets were full of deer and the forest grew denser. The air was purified and there were no vapor trails in the sky. I planted potatoes and caught fish. The river wasn't polluted anymore, and the salmon came leaping. The earth revived when people stopped burdening it with all their garbage. And I got peace to research Obsidiana's story."

"But why didn't you do something when the world was under a spell?"

"I didn't really know at that point whether the world was under a spell or if it had been freed from one. Humanity had destroyed so much. Everybody had been racing against time, trying to accumulate as much stuff as they could. People had ruined everything that was beautiful, but now they were shut inside their own stupidity."

"But what about us? You have to help us get back home."

"It's not up to me. The world will only get better if you make it better. I'm only an old woman."

"What can we do?"

"You need to listen to the story all the way to the end."

Anori

The day following the grand ceremony, Anori roamed the city; the atmosphere was joyful, food was cooking on every corner, and the clamorous streets echoed with a multitude of languages and the sounds of exotic musical instruments. The people were waiting for the princess to be carried onto the square. Anori was perplexed: For a whole year his mind had been on the girl in the casket, first out of remorse for what he had done but later because she was his friend. He longed to tell somebody his secret, but he trusted nobody. He buried the secret deep in his heart. During the king's visit, Anori had seen how happy Obsidiana was when she appeared on the balcony to acknowledge the cheers of the crowd; he felt sure she had seen him standing on top of a column, waving a flag. But now there was a knot in his belly and he didn't know what the future held—would he ever be able to sneak into the palace to meet her again?

He clambered across the rooftops to watch the monks bring Obsidiana to the square—but when she appeared, it was as if a shock wave traveled through the sea of people; cries and howls rose from the crowd, and the festive atmosphere died instantly.

"It's a bad omen! A bad omen!" old women wailed. Anori's heart jolted, and he hurried down to get a closer view. People were swarming into the temple and back out onto the square; the throng swirled round and round like a whirlpool, and a mountain of offerings piled up in the center of the square: exquisite rugs, flour, nuts and dates, gold and glittering jewels.

Pushing his way through the crowd, Anori at last reached the casket. Now he saw Obsidiana. Her face was distorted into a horrible, frozen scowl; her eyes stared, full of spite; and her fingers curled like the claws of a hissing cat. She looked like a demon.

He shuddered and touched the casket, murmuring a prayer like everybody else; he couldn't understand what had happened. He looked at Urchin standing on a rostrum, gesturing as he spoke: "We uncovered a traitor yesterday! The people of the Cloud Mountains in the east have broken their pledge to Pangea. THE GODS ARE ANGRY! THE KING AND HIS ARMY HAVE GONE TO PUNISH THOSE WHO BETRAYED HIM! OBSIDIANA DEMANDS REVENGE! SHE DEMANDS SACRIFICES AND REVENGE!"

Anori felt sick. Something terrible must have happened after they parted. He had to find out—she couldn't have changed into a witch in just twenty-four hours. He waited for an opportunity but, contrary to the usual routine, the monks didn't take her home that evening; the casket remained in the temple all night. Around the princess, fires were lit to project a shadow of her frown and sharpened talons onto the temple wall.

Obsidiana was on display all that week and the following weeks, and the expression on her face never changed. Anori was at his wits' end. He must speak to her! Full moon after full moon came and went. He had to find an opportunity to open the lid and ask her what had happened, but the guards didn't take their eyes off her.

Urchin knew the powerful effect of Obsidiana's new appearance. People listened more closely and gave more. Her expression, and the weather, helped give force to his apocalyptic sermons.

Winds shook the kingdom, there was a hurricane in the east, forest fires in the south, a volcanic eruption in the west—all signs of Obsidiana's and the gods' fury. The king was bound sooner or later to hear about the frown, so Urchin decided to get in first with the news and sent him a crowmail:

> *Most Venerable Majesty! Obsidiana sides with you in your battle and directs the power of the gods toward you! She has adopted an expression that will frighten your enemies and spur the gods of war to action!*

Exel, on the other hand, was not sure that the frown was appropriate for the princess's image, but his calculations showed that gold was flowing into the public purse like never before.

Urchin preached to the masses every day: "THE ETERNAL PRINCESS FROWNS AT YOUR EVIL THOUGHTS! SHE HISSES AT YOUR GREED!"

Men wearing cloaks with a closed eye embroidered on the chest went around the city tearing valuables from the hands of the people.

"More sacrifices!" they demanded.

But few had anything left to give.

Anori tried to stay indoors. His aunt Borghild sighed and hobbled around the house; she lit incense in front of a crudely carved image of the girl.

"Eternal Princess, I don't know what made you so angry. Please give us rain for the wheat. Provide sunshine for the flowers. Provide life for the seeds. Provide food for the boy. Please don't be angry, kind princess. Don't be angry."

She had emptied every last sack and was eking out the oatmeal with twigs and stalks. The meat in the market could be that of any animal—dog, cat, monkey, pigeon, or rat. Rumor had it that somebody had even been selling human flesh.

Anori knew the way to the royal pantry, and that's where he finally headed when no other options remained. He gazed ruefully into the empty room that he had visited every full moon for so long. But the pantry was nearly empty—no potatoes, lamb, or cocoa from the western regions. He took a few morsels of meat, a tiny piece of cheese, and a handful of grain; scarcely enough to live off but enough for survival. It would be suspicious if he looked too well-fed. He was about to hurry back when he heard the creak of a floorboard and the sound of many feet moving about on the wooden floor of the audience chamber above him. By now he knew the castle like the back of his hand, so he was able to find a hiding place from where he could observe what was happening. He peered through a knothole and saw Gunnhild sitting on the throne, looking miserable. Exel sat on her right, and to her left Urchin and the queen's elegantly clothed but grumpy daughters. A young man accompanied by five knights approached the queen's throne. They were good-looking men, handsomely dressed and armed.

"Your Majesty, my name is Orri, I am the son of the Duke of Plains. I bring you gifts from my father and a letter for the king. As you know, my father has been his closest ally for many decades."

"And what can I do for you?" Gunnhild asked warmly.

"I request the hand of the Eternal Princess in marriage."

"I see," she said and smiled. "Did you know that only once in a hundred years is someone born who is worthy of her?"

"Your Majesty, in my favor I should like to mention my prowess in battle and the fact that I know by heart most of the works in your library including all two thousand of the poems in the *Epic of Pangea*. I have led armies and won more battles than anyone else in King Dimon's armies. If it had not been for me all the districts east of Aranandia would be lost to us, an area that now forms the king's mightiest stronghold."

"Do you consider it seemly to ask for the princess's hand in front of my daughters?"

The older daughter smiled faintly and fluttered her eyelashes.

The duke's son blushed. "Your Majesty. I do not mean to disrespect your daughters; it is just that when I was dancing with Obsidiana during the opening ceremony my father discussed this with the king, who said he would be happy for me to ask for her hand in the future when she became, um . . . older. It would strengthen the unity of the empire."

Anori's heart pounded in his breast. He wished he had a bow and arrows so he could shoot the man through the heart.

Gunnhild stared at Orri. "She is still too young," she said. He looked surprised. "How can that be? I am eighteen and she was born long before me."

"In that case, isn't she too old for you?" Gunnhild laughed.

"I can wait for her if she is too young," said Orri humbly. "Three years, six years are no time at all for me."

"Well, it could take her over a hundred years to age three years." She took out a notebook. "How much time would you like?"

"What do you mean?"

"Surely you don't intend to waste all her time and take her with you to the grave?"

"What?"

"You do realize that you cannot be with her every day, don't you? How much time would you like to spend with her?"

"I don't understand what you mean, ma'am."

"We are expecting her to live for thousands of years. Do you think she wants to get married every hundred years?"

Orri scratched his head. This had not occurred to him.

"Do you have any pearls?" Gunnhild asked.

"I have twenty thousand pearls, Your Majesty."

"Exel," said the stepmother, "how much time would that be?"

"That's just over two years, Your Majesty."

"That means you can afford nearly two years of her precious time," Gunnhild said frostily. "They may be spread across one lifetime."

Stony-faced, Urchin whispered something to Gunnhild. She looked back at him, indignant.

"She said that? That is so like her."

"Yes," said Urchin. "Obsidiana says he must prove his worth, and she has a message for him."

"I will accept any challenge," said Orri with a hopeful smile. He brushed a lock of hair from his face and waited for a reply.

"Urchin!" Gunnhild cried. "Tell Orri what the Eternal Princess wants him to do."

Urchin closed his eyes; for a long time he was silent, and when he opened them again only the whites were visible. He murmured:

"Beyond Snake Mountain on the far side of the ocean is a strait full of poisonous jellyfish. Swim across and you will find an old nest belonging to the Golden Crow. Fetch me the eggs of this bird."

Orri's face darkened and he addressed the queen. "Are you serious, Ma'am?"

"Do I have any say in anything?" she said. "You heard it yourself. Urchin has explained her demand. If you'd rather swim across Jellyfish Strait than marry either of my daughters, you may swim to your heart's content!"

"Is this meant to be an insult?"

"Anyone foolhardy enough to swim across Jellyfish Strait should be able to live forever."

"In that case, let it be so!" said the duke's son. He and his knights turned and clomped out of the audience chamber. They rode off and disappeared into the night.

Anori had followed these exchanges intently and repeated in his mind what the queen had said: "We are expecting her to live for thousands of years." "Take her with you to the grave?" Everyone in this palace was going stark raving crazy. Obsidiana had towered above him when they first met, and now they were about as tall as each other. Would he go on to become taller and older than her?

Exel sat deep in thought, tapping away at his calculator, before saying:

"Madam, my calculations show that the probability of his getting across Jellyfish Strait alive is only 0.04%."

"Shut up, bean counter!" Gunnhild hissed. "Do not dare to dispute the will of the gods!"

Exel's face turned white as chalk, and he returned to his calculations. Then he sprang to his feet.

"This is taking things too far! You have just sent our most important ally to his certain death. According to my calculations, this will have a fateful effect on the progress of the war. And why does the princess have this expression on her face? I was given the task of applying precise calculations in order to secure her happiness. Take a look at this report!" He waved a folder at Urchin and Gunnhild.

"These days, fear is the only thing the people understand," Urchin said. "Fear is the only thing that will fill the coffers. Fear keeps the people subdued and stops them from flocking onto the streets and storming the palace in search of food."

"I demand an emergency meeting!" Exel said. "I want a declaration from the king confirming his approval of this course of action!"

"Come with me!" said Urchin and hauled himself off to a tower room, with Exel following. Crows sat on every windowsill with unanswered mail and petitions.

Exel raised his voice to be heard above the cawing: "It is useless to display Obsidiana on the square every day. People can't bring sacrifices all day and night. They aren't bringing any more money! Just take a look at this chart!"

Urchin took a piece of chalk out of his pocket and drew a line across the doorway, then another and another, too close together for a foot to fit between them.

"What are you doing?" said Exel, trembling and quivering. He couldn't get to the door. "Erase these lines!"

But Urchin surrounded Exel with lines so that he was trapped in the middle of the floor.

Urchin laughed and rattled his chains. "Stay there and turn into stone!"

Exel yelled but nobody could hear him. His screams were drowned by the cawing of the crows.

Urchin went around the palace herding together Exel's team of check-suited accountants; he opened the castle gates and said: "Giddy up! Off you go! You're free!"

They filed out with their rulers and spectacles. They walked slowly, gazing fearfully at the cruel, chaotic world that awaited them.

Enantiodromia

The morning sun woke King Dimon. Soon, he was feeling optimistic: Urchin had sent him a morale-boosting message, and it appeared even Obsidiana was in fighting mood and in contact with the gods of war. He had gone outside to breathe some fresh air and spotted a mail crow sitting on his tent. There was a message attached to its leg:

Obsidiana has spoken with the gods. They will be sending you more powers. You should follow the valley to seek reinforcements from the duke. All is well at the palace. According to our calculations Obsidiana is very happy. Respectfully yours, Exel.

King Dimon and his men rode along a grassy valley with a wide river snaking through it. As they finally approached the Western States, they saw soldiers lined up on the surrounding hills and crags to meet them. Having expected a royal reception, Dimon was stirred when the soldiers took up trumpets and began a ceremonial fanfare. He rode on—but there was no welcoming party; what had started as a quiet flourish grew louder as more trumpeters joined in, and the king's good spirits gave way to apprehension when drummers started up a deafening tattoo. The noise became so overpowering that Dimon's men cast aside their shields and weapons and covered their ears. Rhinos went into a frenzy, dragging wagons and trailers behind them until they smashed to pieces. Finally the clamor died down but, as Dimon's men lay on the ground with their ears buzzing, something veiled the light of the sun. A dark shape appeared in the sky, like a cloud of migrating birds.

"ARROWS!" the men yelled, trying to escape—but it was too late. The arrows plunged vertically earthward like gannets diving into a shoal of herrings, piercing dirt, helmets, skin, and bone. Dimon took cover behind a dead rhino, and his copper shield sheltered him from the razor-sharp projectiles that battered the animal's corpse like rain on a tent roof.

When the attack finally died down, Dimon gazed at his fallen troops in horror; lying on the ground, many of them looked like sea urchins, with forests of arrows sticking out of their backs. He picked up an arrow and saw his own coat of arms carved into the wood. The words of the old woman on the ice sounded again in his ears: "No one conquers the world who cannot conquer time!"

"THIS IS BETRAYAL!" Dimon yelled, so loud that he made the mountains reverberate. "It was I who had these arrows made! It was I who had them sent here! It was I who trained the troops! THIS IS MY ARMY! DON'T YOU DARE USE MY OWN WEAPONS AGAINST ME!" As his words rang around the hills, the echo seemed to be saying to him: "How did I dare to set the animals against people?"

Dimon looked up and saw a catapult being wound up on one of the hills. Soon something flew toward him. He jumped aside as a man landed with a splat at his feet. It was a messenger with a note tied to his leg.

Dear Dimon. Thank you for your long-standing friendship. This welcome is most fitting for the man who ordered my son Orri to swim across Jellyfish Strait.

Dimon was flabbergasted.

"That's nonsense! I never told him to swim anywhere. Last time I saw Orri he was dancing at the opening ceremony."

"Fall in for inspection!" he yelled, but his sergeant major didn't respond; he had eighteen arrows sticking out of his back. The blizzard of arrows had been so thick that the area looked like a field of wheat. Dimon wandered around the battlefield, his shoulders hunched like an old farmer checking his harvest. He found Consiglio under a tree and plucked two arrows from his thigh and one from his shoulder, bound his wounds, and helped him to his feet. Between them they managed to patch together the remnants of the army; they collected swords and helmets and gathered the dead together and burned them.

As they retreated through a pass, men atop one of the hills showered them with flaming rocks that crushed heads and broke horses' backs. Soldiers in flames ran around screaming. Dimon hid beneath an elephant carcass as the boulders crashed around him. At the height of the onslaught he thought he saw an old woman with a twisted narwhal tooth leaping about. He ground his teeth so hard that he splintered his molars. He wrote a letter home and tied it to a crow's foot:

Dear daughter, we are moving slowly toward our goal. Soon Pangea's sun of victory will shine again!

With much love, Dad.

While the king was scribbling these words of optimism, back home Chief Accountant Exel was trapped in the crow tower. He gazed in panic at all the lines drawn around him. They were dense and scary, like a spider's web. He tried to step onto the lines but couldn't do it; his body stiffened, and his feet refused to obey him. He tried to capture the attention of the guards by waving and jumping, but he faded so well into the gray of the walls that no one could see him. He tapped figures into his calculator and realized that he would die of hunger and thirst if he were unable to get out. He took a piece of paper and wrote a message to the king, which he attached to a crow's foot and sent off:

System failure at the palace; strengths are minimal, threats many, opportunities few. The corners of the princess's mouth are turned down, indicating unhappiness. Urchin and Gunnhild are turning your allies against you. Results of my calculations indicate they would like you dead.

Exel had nothing to reward the crow with, so he pricked his finger and gave it a tiny drop of blood. The crow cawed happily and flew off. Exel was hot, thirsty, and hungry. He tried to kill time by calculating the volume of the room; the ceiling was conical so the calculation was a little complicated. And then he remembered the good old days when he sat in this very same tower and taught the crows to fetch gold. Exel whispered the goldcrow rhyme that had brought such great wealth to the state back then. The crows fell silent, turned their heads this way and that, and made themselves scarce. They returned that evening in their thousands with a glittering treasure.

This made Exel very happy and he began to count up the pickings. By evening the gold reached his shoulders and before he knew it he was buried up to his neck. He tried to tell the birds to stop but couldn't remember the last verse, and with no haggis to reward them, the crows perched on his head and began to peck.

The Abandoned Toy Store

Listening to Grace's story, Marcus had gotten worried. As crows gathered, squawking, in the tree outside, he thought about his friends, his brothers and sisters, and the girl he had a crush on. He thought, too, about his grandmother and grandfather, the ones who lived in the north. Was everyone frozen inside boxes up there as well? Were cities all over the world like this? How was it possible that everybody had decided to escape from time? Absolutely everybody!

"Excuse me," he said politely, "but we can't just sit here listening to a story. We have to do something right away."

"I've already tried," said Grace. "Let me just finish the story."

"It must be possible for us to open the caskets and let people out."

Grace sighed and looked at the clock. "Okay, we can take a short break." She reached into her handbag, fished out an Allen wrench, and handed it to him.

"Take this. Open any casket you want to."

"You have an Allen wrench?"

"Of course."

"And I can open any casket I want to?"

"More or less."

"Great! Who's coming with me?" said Marcus with a sense of hope, pulling his shoes on.

"I'll come!" said Sigrun eagerly.

"I'll start to read again in two hours," said Grace.

Sigrun and Marcus ran off, wondering who might have the answers. Sigrun looked around and spotted the parliament building, covered with briars and thorns.

"Grace said we could open up and release anyone at all," Sigrun said. "The politicians must know what happened."

The entrance door stood ajar, and they peered into a long, marble-clad corridor. Bits of paper swirled around in the draft like leaves in fall. On one wall there were busts and paintings of cabinet ministers, all coated with dust. The ministers themselves were lined up along the opposite wall, bathed in blueish light. Marcus examined the caskets and, spotting someone he recognized from television news programs, inserted the Allen wrench into the lock and opened the casket.

"Why are you bothering me?" the man asked grumpily. He wore a slate-gray suit and looked tired.

"You're a cabinet minister, aren't you?" Marcus asked.

"I don't know. What year is it now?" The man looked at a meter on the casket and heaved a sigh of relief. "No, I'm not a minister, and I'm not responsible for anything."

"Aren't you?" said Marcus. "It says cabinet minister on the casket."

"No, the term of office is over," he said, removing the label that showed his job title. "Well, goodbye then," he added. "I'm not coming out until the financial system has recovered."

"And when will that be?"

The man shrugged. "When the situation improves. But right now I'm exhausted. It's been a very difficult term." He pointed at another casket. "Talk to the opposition, they always pretend to have all the answers."

He slammed his lid shut. The kids went over to a casket containing a middle-aged woman in a suit; she stood bolt upright with a steely expression. Sigrun opened the casket.

"What?" asked the woman. "What year is it now?" She looked at the clock. "Right. The term is over at last. What's the situation like?"

"Everything's in total chaos," said Marcus. "The situation is very grave."

"Of course!" said the woman triumphantly. "Just as I said would happen. Don't point the finger at me. I didn't have a hand in anything, I was in here all the time, and I'm absolutely not going to mop up the mess the last administration left behind!"

"But someone has to do something," Sigrun said.

"Yes, but what happens if I do the mopping? As soon as everything's back to normal the previous idiots will be re-elected. You mark my words!"

"Come on," Marcus whispered. "This is useless." The woman slammed her casket shut. Marcus and Sigrun hastened to the nursing home, where they found Marcus's grandmother in a casket stacked in a cubby.

"Hello, Marcus dear," she said.

"Grammy, you have to help me. Everybody in the world has disappeared!"

"I know all about that, my little buddy."

"Help us. We have to get everyone out of the caskets before it's too late. Come with us, Grammy! You remember what time was like in the olden days."

"Oh, I'm not sure," she said.

"Pretty please?" Out the window they could see a wall with faded slogans:

DO YOU WANT THE CRISIS TO HARM YOUR KIDS?
TimeBox®

WIND AND RAIN FORECAST FOR ALL NEXT YEAR!
TimeBox®

ARE THE WORST YEARS OF YOUR LIFE AHEAD?
TimeBox®

"I don't have many good years left, Marcus dear. I was born during the Great Depression and I don't want to spend my last years in that sort of misery."

"But Grammy, we'll open more caskets. We'll get people together and start up a little community, and then we'll get more people to join in."

"Humph! You're starting to think like one of those hippies!" The room was not heated; his grandmother shivered and eyed the wallpaper flapping on the walls.

"Is the café on the corner open?" she said.

"No," Marcus said.

"Your plan won't work, Marcus dear. Just hurry back home."

Sigrun and Marcus left the nursing home and went to call on their friends.

"Hi! Do you want to come out?" But the answer was always the same. Their friends looked fearfully out at the world and said timidly: "No, I'm not allowed to. It's too dangerous out there, and I promised Mom I'd wait at home."

They found the baker.

"Good morning, can you please open the bakery again?"

"There's nobody here to bake for."

They found a doctor.

"There are no patients, and the golf course is overgrown."

Sigrun was intending to open her parents' caskets. She stood in front of them with the Allen wrench, but then put it back in her pocket.

"They're sure to force me to get back into my box," she said sadly; she left, fighting back tears.

They went past an abandoned store with Magni's Toy Store written on the window. Next to it was an enormous hand-painted sign:

NOW IN STORE: FEBRUARY GAMES!
Kites! Beach Spades! Rainsuits!

Marcus tried the door and found it unlocked. Inside, the air was stuffy, and they saw shelves laden with dust-covered dolls and teddy bears, yellowed toy boxes, remote control model planes, cars, and dolls' strollers. In the stockroom an older man stood like a frozen mannequin in a black box surrounded by dusty model aircraft and jigsaw puzzles.

Scattered all around were paint pots and signs with faded lettering:

EVERY DAY IS AN ADVENTURE
IMAGINATION CONQUERS TIME!

They heard a voice behind them. Grace had joined them. "He was the last one," she said. "He'd made signs to hang up all around the city."

The kids examined the signs.

GOOD TIMES AHEAD
A BIG MESS = PLENTY OF WORK!

"He was an optimist, but, after a whole year as the only person left in the city, he closed the store and got himself a casket."

"This is ridiculous," Sigrun said. "Marcus's grandma won't come out until a café has been opened; the politician won't clear up the mess the previous administration left behind; the kids are too scared to come out and play. They've all gone completely out of their minds."

"The thing is," Grace said, "the caskets make it so easy to postpone time. It's so easy to put off solving your problems—it's just like having someone pinch you nice and gently."

"So it's the people themselves that are deciding this is how the world should be?"

"In a way," Grace said.

"Is there nothing that can be done?"

"Well, I think there might be. Let's finish the story."

Run Boy!

Anori snuck home with some food for his aunt. Borghild was panic-stricken when she saw him at the door; she hurried him inside and whispered:

"You must go away! There were men here earlier, looking for you. They searched all over the house. I don't know who they were. Most of the boys on the street have been drafted, even ones younger than you. Those who end up being sent home injured are the lucky ones. You must run away!"

"Where to? Where?"

"You're fourteen years old, Anori, you're almost grown-up. Try to go up north. Try to get to the countries Dimon has lost. There's peace there! Now, hurry—go!"

"What about Dad?"

"It's no use waiting for the war to be over. You must go!"

"But who'll look after you?"

"Don't you worry about me, I'll be alright." Hastily, Anori got some food and clothes together. He saw that the shrine had disappeared; the little altar dedicated to the Eternal Princess was no longer there.

"Where's the shrine?" he said. "Where's Obsidiana's picture?"

"That fiend?" Borghild spat. "Don't mention her name in our house! Now go. Go as far as you can! This city is no place for boys your age."

She opened a little box and fished out an elephant carved from whalebone. One eye was formed of a blue stone inside of which was a tiny red drop; the other eye was missing. She handed it to Anori.

"This belonged to your grandmother, my sister. The king's guards came for her when your dad was a tiny baby, and she never returned home."

She gave him a big, long hug. "Take care of yourself." They both shed tears, and Anori left. But instead of running away from the city he headed off to the palace, found the rabbit hole, and crept directly up to the chamber where the casket had been. He had to find out what had happened. Sooner or later the princess would surely be carried back here. He holed up in the back room with the broken spiral staircase, behind the little hatch, where he swept away the dust and made a den for himself.

The days passed slowly; he sought out nooks and crannies where he could sit for days on end and spy on court life, and sometimes he descended into the vaults to practice shooting with a bow and arrows that he'd found in an ancient armory. Often he lay atop the old watchtower gazing at the stars slowly revolving overhead. At night the city was silent, with fewer fires and no one singing; the only sounds were of the guards driving stray dogs away.

Anori soon got to know everything that went on in the castle. He knew all about the changing of the guard, and he knew that the two sisters were moody in the evenings. One regularly sneaked out to meet one of the guards, while the other seemed to have gone a bit weird, sitting on her bed muttering to herself. As for Gunnhild, she paced the corridors like a caged lion. Anori overheard their conversations when Urchin brought her messages from Obsidiana:

"She is not happy with you today. You must be careful with your thoughts or she will bad-mouth you to the gods."

Anori learned to move along ceiling joists in the dark; he had familiarized himself with all the castle's cavities and voids and found crevices where he could hide the whole day without being seen. He loved watching the court artists, how they handled their brushes, stretched canvases, drew lines, painted the base coat, and then added a layer and another layer, and how they mixed powders of many colors to make paint. It fascinated him to see how faces appeared in the pictures, along with horses and mountains, ships and epic battles.

At night, he snuck out from hiding to study the paintings up close. Here was scaffolding in front of half-finished pictures of the kingdom in all its glory; here was a picture of King Dimon surrounded by soldiers and animals, evidently painted before the empire split into two; here was Dimon with a chain over his shoulder, heaving a rock that symbolized the Great Rift—Anori comforted himself by imagining that the soldier standing behind the king with a bow and arrows was his dad. Here were pictures of the check-suited Exel; and here somebody had started painting a picture of the beautiful Obsidiana in her glass casket. Behind her you could see the outlines of the king, the queen, and the two sisters. Obsidiana's face was almost complete, but it didn't look like her at all. *I would have done a better job of painting her*, Anori thought.

He filled a bag with brushes and paint, and crept back to his lair, where he fastened a thick coverlet over the window so he could light the room with candles at nighttime. He looked at the stone-gray walls and reflected on the time that had passed since he first came here as a little boy; he thought about the stories that Obsidiana had told him and set about making them come alive on the walls around his squalid bed. He painted a picture of Obsidiana holding a giant goldfish with two small deer at her feet. All through that winter and into spring he painted, becoming more and more accomplished as time went by. He drew white birds and birds of prey and crows on a tower. Then he moved around to the next wall, where he painted a whole forest full of strange animals, a red panda, and a one-eyed elephant. Next he decorated the ceiling with a blue sky and clouds, and in one corner he painted a sledgehammer and a broken casket, with time caressing Obsidiana like a fresh breeze; judging by the look on her face, she was free.

The days went by. Anori had become pale as a sheet from always being indoors; he ventured nowhere except to fetch food and more paints, and his only companion was a rat whom he allowed to nibble at his leftovers. He took immense care as he crept around the castle—one false step would mean death for him. Visiting the court artists' studio one night, he took a closer look at a painting of Obsidiana; he studied it, shook his head, and got some paint. He dabbed a brushstroke of white to the nose, gave a shine to her hair, and adjusted the corner of one eye. He added a twinkle to her gaze, made her lips a little redder, broadened her forehead, and added shadows to match the sun's position in the picture. When the artist returned next morning, Obsidiana's perfect face shone out of the canvas. It was evident that mysterious forces had been at work.

They're Back!

Painting helped Anori to forget about time and the fact that he couldn't get to Obsidiana. But one day he heard orders being shouted at the guards:

"Red alert this evening! The casket will be opened and the princess will appear before the people!"

Anori's heart jumped. He had to get to the square. The streets were not safe, so he scrambled over the rooftops to where he could glimpse the casket in its place in the temple. He was disheartened by the terrible look on Obsidiana's face, which almost radiated darkness. He had to do something—but what? He missed her so.

The bell in the temple rang out and palace guards herded the citizens onto the square. The monks fetched the casket and bore it ceremonially up to the balcony, where they stood it upright. His chains rattling, Urchin approached the casket and opened it with a theatrical gesture, unleashing Obsidiana's scowl, which turned into a scream—a piercing, terrible scream that pulsed through the city like an icy shiver.

"Step forward," Urchin said. Obsidiana screwed up her eyes. The people shuddered. Just look at that deathly white face and those bloodthirsty lips! She looked around, her eyes still brimming with anger and hate. Anori couldn't move; his heart hammered in his chest. What had happened? He had never seen her so full of evil.

Urchin raised his arms up high. "Does anyone wish to feel her anger?" Obsidiana screamed at him. A flock of mail crows took to the air and circled around the towers. CAW! CAW! CAW! The people were seized with panic. Children howled and women wailed as the guards passed through the crowd seizing bread, grains, clothing, and finery. Obsidiana had become a symbol for tyranny and oppression, injustice and greed. She was still screeching as the monks closed the casket lid, freezing her face in a silent scream. Immediately, the mob started pushing and shoving in the square, causing a massive stampede.

Anori was about to retreat from the roof when he suddenly found himself cornered by three men.

"Loathsome witch," said the oldest of them, spitting in her direction.

Anori froze. It was a familiar voice.

"Where've you been hiding, kid? We've been looking for you a long time."

They looked him up and down. "Paint stains? Where'd you get those?"

"I broke into an artist's house," Anori said. "But he didn't have anything valuable. What do you want?"

"Come with us." They shunted Anori ahead of them, down from the roof and through the streets until they arrived at a wretched inn; the air inside stank like a sleeping drunkard. The guy who seemed to be their leader was smoking a pipe—although it was supposed to be impossible to get hold of tobacco after the loss of Pangea's western half.

"You've grown, buddy." Anori looked round; it was the man who had made him crawl into the grave, now sporting a full beard.

"Yeah," said Anori. "Kids grow."

"You're pale, but you look healthy. Where d'you get your food?" the man said, pinching the flesh of Anori's arm.

"I manage," said Anori, sweating. Did they know anything? The man laughed at his reaction and slapped him on the back.

"You take care of yourself. You're resourceful. I like that. We need people like you." Anori was downcast. "Don't act so miserable, kid," the man said roughly. "We didn't treat you so bad back in the day, did we? Eh? Didn't make you do anything we hadn't done ourselves sometime. You did well for us. Recognize this sword?" He drew his sword from its scabbard and showed it to Anori. "This has killed many a man since you got it for me. You were like a little monkey when you climbed into that merchant's place," he said, stroking the sharp blade.

"What do you want?" Anori said. The man suddenly looked serious.

"We've been looking for you. We have information about what happened to your father."

Anori was startled.

"Your father was killed in a battle."

Anori grew pale. "No! That can't be right!"

"Dimon censors all news of casualties, but we know the truth." The man was gentler than before, almost sympathetic, and gripped Anori's shoulder warmly.

"We have a witness who was in the same unit when he was killed in the Cliff Pass action."

"Why should I believe you?"

"They lie to keep up the illusion," said a voice behind him; it came from a one-armed man standing in the shadows. "They knew the battle was lost but they still sent us forward. My son and three of my brothers died there, and I saw when your father was killed. He was a solid guy, your dad."

181

"No!" Anori said. "You're lying!"

"We have the casualty list here," said the leader. "We filched it from the king's encampment." He leafed through the document and pointed at one of a long list of names.

That was when Anori passed out.

Rebels

Anori woke to find himself in a comfortable bed. A kindly woman offered him milk to drink, saying: "You must have been hungry and tired."

He got up and looked around. It was a cozy place with a fire crackling in the hearth; there were some boys of his own age, and a few older men talking in low voices. More men came in, and the woman greeted them warmly:

"You're safe and sound!"

"Yes, Mom," said one of the new arrivals. With his mop of red hair and green eyes he looked like his mother, and his voice was familiar to Anori. He had been one of the gang who made him climb into the merchant's house. The woman served supper. It had been ages since Anori had sat down for a meal by a crackling fire, and he eagerly wolfed down rice and beetroot soup containing some good chunks of meat.

The men at the end of the table were having a discussion: "I trust that nothing said here will go beyond these walls; I trust that you will swear this on the memory of your fathers and brothers. Dimon the Cruel has reached the end of his journey. His evildoing must cease. There is hardly a person on this earth who has not suffered because of his actions. He turned the animals against the people and sacrificed the lives of thousands."

"Shush!" said the woman. "Don't talk like that. Walls have ears."

"Not anymore," the man said. "The guards are too scared to take us on. We know where they live." He raised his voice as if in warning to any spy that might be listening and turned toward Anori: "Dimon is a monster, and his daughter is even worse."

"I've heard that she wanders around at night with a devil they call the Black Prince," another said.

Anori pricked up his ears. "Huh? Black what?"

"The Black Prince. They were first seen together on the square some years back, and they've been sighted prowling around the palace at full moon."

Anori broke out in a cold sweat and swallowed. Had someone spotted them in the palace?

"I've heard horror stories about them," the woman said. "One time, an unknown girl turned up at a farm and asked the wife to look after her little baby. The woman took it in and put it in the crib with her own child, but later that night she heard greedy munching noises, and when she went to check on the crib she found it was no baby but an evil creature that had devoured every last morsel of her child. The creature looked at her and hissed; the woman said it was the same look we've seen on the square. It was them! Obsidiana and the Black Prince."

"Bullshit!" said Anori, but immediately regretted opening his mouth.

The men fell silent and looked at him. The woman laughed: "Well, well! You've gotten used to worshipping her, haven't you?"

"What we've seen with our own eyes is far worse than the stories," the red-haired guy said. "The king's evil accountant Exel calculates how to wipe out whole nations. To him, women and children are nothing but numbers. He was the one who had the king break the promise not to set animals against people."

Pouring hot water into a teapot, he went on: "I know this from my own experience. My grandfather Michael made the statue that stands on the square. He was a great artist and thought he could preserve Obsidiana's beauty forever, but the king was furious when he saw that it said 'Michael Hoggmin' on the plinth rather than 'Obsidiana,' and had him thrown to the lions. Dimon was crazy many decades ago, but he is twice as bad now."

Another man stepped out from the shadows: "I was in the battalion that passed through the Golden City a few weeks after Dimon's men had campaigned there. It was horrifying. Hyenas still roamed around devouring what was left of the people. We found a little baby alive, starving and looking like a frightened puppy. I'll never forget it."

"The victories were even more dreadful than the defeats," added another.

They sat silent a while. Then they looked at Anori. "We need you."

"Yeah?" Anori tried to swallow a piece of bread but his throat was dry; the woman replenished the milk in his glass.

"Dimon's reign of terror has gone on long enough; Dimon and the princess will not live to see the next full moon!"

Anori choked on his milk. The men who had been sitting quietly next to the leader became uneasy.

"You talk too loud," one whispered.

"Relax," the man said.

"The palace will catch wind of this."

"And who here plans to squeal?" The man looked around menacingly. "Anyone remember Finn? You know what happens to blabbermouths!" He turned sharply to Anori: "Same applies to you, too. You can climb, and that's why we need you. Just remember who caused your father's death. Be ready. We'll come for you."

"When?" Anori asked.

"Only spies ask questions like that," the man said, looking threateningly at him. He dug out a battered map: an old drawing of the palace with possible entry routes marked on it.

"On the seaward side of the castle it's possible to climb up unobserved. There's an abandoned watchtower here," he said, pointing at the map. "It used to be inaccessible, but in recent years it's gotten overgrown with thorns. Someone not too heavy could climb up and reach this window here. From that point there's a corridor that leads to here, where the casket is." He pointed at the room that Anori knew so well.

Anori had to restrain himself. He knew the palace like the back of his hand and could see this was an out-of-date map; the door they were planning to use had been bricked up. He kept quiet so as not to give them any helpful ideas, but the potential route using the thorns surprised him, and he became worried. Obsidiana was evidently not safe in the castle.

The man continued: "This is a job for two guys. You need to help each other climbing up the thorns. From there you go along the corridor to the princess's room. That's when you need to work real fast."

"We? You want me to climb up to her room?" Anori asked.

"You can climb. You've burrowed into graves. You can do this. You and him."

He pointed at the red-haired guy with the green eyes. "He's young, but he's used a knife."

"A knife?" said Anori.

"You rip the casket open, and he stabs her in the heart. Make sure you don't look into her eyes, she could curse you."

Anori stared at the map, chilled to his core. "Stab her?"

"Ridding the world of the princess is the easiest way to dethrone Dimon. She's a monster. She's responsible for the indescribable suffering the world has had to endure, and for your father's death, too. You scared? You think you can do this?"

Anori nodded slowly. "I can do it."

The men went into a corner and conferred in whispers. Anori looked around at the people sitting there eating, mending their clothes, sharpening swords. He had a tight knot in his stomach. The man returned.

"You want to stay here? Do you have somewhere?"

"No, I'm fine, I've got a place to sleep," Anori said.

"We'll give you a sign," the man said. "Keep your mouth shut, even if they pull your nails out. It'll be easier to get at her inside the castle than out on the square—that would cost us fifty people, but inside the castle we'd sacrifice no more than two."

"Sacrifice two?"

"Avenging your father comes with risks. We're promising nothing, and anything can happen. Be unobtrusive. They'll carry Obsidiana into the castle tonight, and we know she'll be there for the next few days."

Anori went out into the night. It was cloudy, and there were no stars or moon to show him the way as he crept along the narrow lanes, making sure nobody was on his tail. When he finally made it into the rabbit hole he lay down on the floor and wept. His dad would not be coming back; King Dimon had sent him to certain death. Obsidiana was trapped in the casket like a screaming witch and the rebels wanted him to kill her. His world was falling apart.

When he reached the back room, Anori heard voices coming from Obsidiana's room. He stopped to listen.

"Just look at her scream," Urchin was saying. "A violent, frozen scream."

Gunnhild said nothing.

"You're quiet," Urchin said.

"I don't have to say anything. She reads my thoughts."

"You were so beautiful. I don't understand why the king lets time ravage you so mercilessly. He lets your beauty slip away when the casket could have preserved your youthful loveliness."

"Dimon doesn't think about me."

"No, he doesn't care about you or your daughters, he thinks only of power. He who has the casket can conquer time and control the people."

Gunnhild didn't reply. "You're silent," said Urchin.

"Yes, you know what I'm thinking." Urchin's chains rattled as he moved closer to her. "I sense it plainly. You hate her. You feel that you should have the casket for yourself."

Still Gunnhild did not respond. "You long for eternal beauty." She stormed out of the room. Left behind, Urchin stroked the lid of the casket and chanted: "'You are so very fine, fine, soon you will be mine, mine.'" He left the chamber, slamming the door.

Anori waited until all was completely silent, and then crawled through the hatch and crept over to the casket to examine Obsidiana's frown close up. Her eyes were screwed up like a cat's and her teeth glistened white like a predator's. What had she been thinking when time stopped? Had she actually become an ogre? He lifted the lid and the princess's fury came alive.

Obsidiana and Anori

Obsidiana hissed. Anori jumped back.

"Hush! It's me!" he whispered. Obsidiana glanced quickly around, and then flung herself into his arms.

"ANORI! You've come! Tell me the news from the world of time!"

She felt a strange feeling stirring in her chest. She wondered whether feelings could simmer inside the casket despite everything else standing still. She had missed Anori. She looked at him.

"What?" he asked.

She reached out and touched his nose. "Your nose has grown so big and your voice has changed!" He blushed and covered his nose with his hand. She squeezed his cheeks. "There's a scar here," she said, stroking the back of his hand. "And here, too. Your ear looks like a wildcat's."

"I was in a fight," he said. "Come on, we don't have time to talk!"

"Stand up straight, let me see you—you're so tall!"

"Sh! Come on, we've no time to lose." He tugged at her.

"How long is it since we saw each other?"

"The opening ceremony, two years ago."

"I don't believe you!" Obsidiana said, frowning again. "How could you do this to me? You promised you'd come!"

"I tried, but for ages Urchin ordered you kept in the temple day and night, so it was impossible to reach you. Come on now, hurry!"

Obsidiana paused a moment before saying: "But what about my father?"

"He's still at war."

"And how's that going?"

"My father never came home. I just learned he was killed in battle."

"Oh," she whispered. "How sad."

"We must go, Obsidiana. We have no choice! The rebels want you dead."

"Who?"

"You don't know them. They think you're a witch. Urchin and the queen want to harm you. They have been undermining the king. Come on!"

Anori tried to drag her toward the hatch behind the drapes.

"No! I want to know what's been happening," she whispered. Becoming more and more impatient, he continued to tug at her as he quickly explained:

"Orri, the Duke of Plains' son, asked for your hand in marriage."

"What?" she said. "He did?"

"Yes, but Urchin read your thoughts; you said he wasn't good enough for you unless he swam across Jellyfish Strait."

Obsidiana looked at him in disbelief. "That's not true!"

"He drowned, and the duke took his revenge, very nearly killing the king in an attack."

Obsidiana was stunned. "Where is he now?"

"The news reports are vague. The king had notices put up all over the city that Pangea should prepare for better times—that soon all would be fixed."

"And is that true?"

"No, the world is falling apart. You spent two years in the temple, and the palace is not safe anymore. We must get away now. Hurry!"

"Dad must come back home before it's too late."

Anori didn't say anything for a moment, but then replied: "Are you sure that's a good idea?"

"What do you mean?"

"Do you think everything will get better then?"

"Of course! He's the king."

Anori shook his head and said: "He imprisoned you in the magic casket! People are afraid of him, and the world is perishing because of him!"

Obsidiana glared angrily at Anori. "Why do you talk like that? If he isn't kind, who is?"

"Maybe no one, but it's the king's fault that my dad died along with thousands of others! He destroys all he comes near. He torches cities and shows no mercy. It was he who set the animals against the people!" Anori clenched his fist, almost ready to explode. "We have to go now! You're in danger! Do you understand?"

Obsidiana closed her eyes, lost in confusion. It was such a short while ago that she had sat in the palace gardens and everything had been wonderful—Peak and Moon came skipping along when she called them, her nurse brought her cookies and milk, her panda snuggled up to her, and Pangea was the greatest empire in the world. It was such a short while ago that she waited impatiently for those letters from her father with pictures of shining turrets. He must be on his way home now.

She looked at the casket, sensing how cold and unforgiving the time was that now enveloped her. It was so tempting to just let it disappear. In a moment everything might be fine again. She went over to the casket.

"But what if I wait here until everything is okay again?"

"Then you will be killed! Urchin has evil plans, and rebels are planning to dethrone the king. If you go back into the casket, the next moment will be your last."

Obsidiana closed her eyes. Anori shook his head. "Do you understand what I'm saying? You'll never see me again if you don't come now." He hurried toward the hole in the wall.

"Wait!" she said. "Wait for me!" She followed him through the hatch and into the room where he had been in hiding for two years. She stopped and gazed in fascination at the walls—at paintings of flowers, a castle and crows, a broken casket, and her with an enormous goldfish in her arms. She moved from painting to painting, touching them. "Did you do these?" she asked. He didn't reply. She moved along the walls, past green meadows, unicorns, and magic ponds to where the two of them stood in front of a magnificent palace with a distant mountain in the background.

"It's so weird," she said, "but I think the casket leaks. I missed you as if a whole eternity had passed."

She held her palm against his and saw that his hand was now bigger than hers.

"We have to go," Anori said. "We have to hurry."

"Sit down, Anori, now it's my turn to tell you a story."

"No, later, we don't have time."

"Yes, now," she said.

192

The Girl in the Casket of Time

"Once upon a time there was a princess who lay in a casket, still and demure, for many years. One day she woke to find a little boy trying to strangle her."

"I know this story," said Anori with a half-smile.

"The whole nation worshipped the girl in the casket, thinking she was a goddess. The more people that saw her, the more important she became, and the more important she became the more people wanted to see her. She was so important that even New Year celebrations were not good enough for her, so precious was her time thought to be. But the boy accidentally let her out in the middle of the night and the girl put a spell on him. He was to come each new moon and bring her news from the outside world. The boy came to her once a month and freed her from the casket. They went on expeditions to see the city and secret places in the castle. But while he grew and developed, she lay in the magic casket like a little seed.

"The girl had never had friends before, but suddenly the boy had become the best friend one could possibly have. She had this strange feeling that, because she met him, everything that had happened to her must have been good."

Anori blushed. Obsidiana put a finger to his lips. "But then she discovered something sad. The first time she met the boy he was nine years old, but only a few days later, or so it seemed to her, he was ten; and then suddenly fourteen. He had become five years older while she had aged just a few days. If this were to continue, he would become eighteen—twenty, forty, fifty—while she was still fourteen. In the end he would die, like all the people she knew. She had come to understand that she didn't want to be the Eternal Princess, she wanted to be the princess in the rain and the snow and the wind and the spring and the winter and the fall. She wanted to see the gray days so she could understand the sunny ones."

"So what did she do?"

"Her father had once given her a secret letter that she might only open in time of dire distress. The letter gave instructions on how to find a cottage by a little lake in the forest, where her mother lay buried. They would be safe there. One day they decided to leave, and they fled there together."

Anori smiled. "And what happened to the princess and the boy?"

"They had five beautiful children."

"Oh?" Anori said and blushed. "I thought they were just good friends."

"Please!" she said. "It's only a fairy tale. They caught trout in the pond; they domesticated two cows and a tiger; squirrels brought them nuts, and moles brought potatoes; and they ate as many pigeons and chicken as they fancied."

"Oh yeah, and is that a life fit for a princess?" Anori laughed.

"Yes," she said. "and in the end they became really old and totally ugly. He got a face as lined as a wrinkled shirt, while she developed a wide butt, an upturned nose, and hair that stuck out in all directions like a dandelion clock. When she laughed you could see her toothless gums, which really scared their grandchildren."

Anori laughed.

"They got so wrinkled that their foreheads stuck together when they kissed!"

Anori laughed even more. "This was a lovely story," he said. Then, becoming serious once more, he added: "But we must get moving—our lives are in danger!"

Obsidiana grasped his hands. "I know of a place," she said. "The little lake where my mother rests. Nobody is allowed there. Nobody but the king knows the way there. He gave me that letter many years ago. Now is the right time to open it."

She took out a worn-looking envelope, securely closed with a seal.

Escape

Anori and Obsidiana gathered everything they could possibly carry: a spade, a fishing rod, an ax, a rug, a tablecloth, two saucepans, a kitchen knife, a large slab of butter, some dried fruit, and some rice, all of which they bundled up in backpacks. They prepared to sneak away in the dead of night, when there was likely to be least danger.

"Do you have everything?" Anori asked. "Let's go!"

He stepped out onto the central column of the spiral staircase, but Obsidiana looked back and said: "Will I never see this place again, then?"

"Not any time soon," said Anori. "Maybe never."

Obsidiana hesitated. "I just have one visit to make first," she said, darting off.

"Where to? We don't have time!"

"I have to say goodbye to my nurse!"

Anori sighed. "We must be quick, then."

He followed Obsidiana, stopping her as they drew near a soldier standing guard over the hall that led to the servants' quarters; powerfully built and armed with a massive spear, the soldier gazed into the darkness like an owl.

"We can't get past him, he never sleeps," said Anori. "I've watched him."

Obsidiana thought a moment and then took a deep breath, straightened her dress, and brushed a lock of hair from her face.

"Follow me," she said.

"What are you going to do?"

"Light the torch."

"Are you crazy? We'll give ourselves away! Come back," Anori pleaded. But she stepped forward, saying: "Do you know who he is?"

"Yeah, his name's Manston."

"What's his mother's name?"

"Josephine."

"Is he married?"

"Yes, to Freya."

"Any children?"

"No."

She tied a piece of black cloth over Anori's head, with a narrow slit for his eyes.

"What's this for?" he asked.

"If they really worship me or if they really fear me then they will do as I say. Follow me!"

She grasped the flaming torch and began to walk straight down the center of the windowless corridor, their shadows flickering on the walls, to where the sentry stood before an ivory door.

"STOP! Who goes there?"

Obsidiana continued confidently toward the guard, who brandished his spear and peered at her through the darkness. He was thunderstruck when he realized it was the princess and the Black Prince; he shivered and shook as Obsidiana glowered and hissed at him.

"Manston. Are you guardsman Manston?" she whispered. He cowered before her.

"Mighty princess, what do you want of me?" A puddle formed at his feet.

"You have been chosen. I have sat with the gods and observed you since you were a child. In the name of your mother Josephine, in the name of your wife Freya, you are to undertake an important task."

"Anything for Your Highness! Anything for Your Highness!" he sobbed.

"You are to open this door and not let anybody know. The Black Prince is with me; he punishes all who do not obey."

Manston instantly straightened up and, with some effort, opened the door.

"Quietly!" Obsidiana hissed. "Now stand guard. Do not dare to follow us!"

She strode onward to the next guard. "Wait here!" she commanded. He prostrated himself at her feet.

They came to a door that opened onto a little courtyard with staging on three sides, lit by a thin paper lantern. An old woman with a gray braid sat on a stool knitting a tiny sock; she looked up as they approached, her eyes gentle but somewhat vacant, her face carved with deep wrinkles. When she saw Obsidiana she smiled a toothless smile:

"Well, well, is it really you?"

"Yes, it's me, dear Thordis."

"So you've come back?"

"Yes, I've come back."

"What's your name?"

"Obsidiana."

"Well," she said, "I have a little girl named Obsidiana. I'm knitting socks for her. She's in the palace gardens with her little deer."

"They are beautiful socks," said Obsidiana, clutching her nurse's hand tightly.

Anori was uneasy; time was running out. The two guards still lay prostrate where they'd left them, but he knew this was playing with fire.

"Thank you, my darling mother," Obsidiana said. "I never said this to you before, but you were the best mother I could have had."

There was a tiny glimmer of comprehension in the old nursemaid's eyes, and she squeezed Obsidiana's hand. A little tear trickled down her cheek as Obsidiana embraced her.

"There, there," Obsidiana said. "Everything will be alright." Anori was about to make a move when he spotted a ring on Thordis's finger. He went over to her, mesmerized. The ring had a blue stone with a red drop in it, just like the eye of the little elephant his aunt had given him. There was no mistake, the stones were identical. He took Thordis's hand and said:

"Do you have a sister named Borghild?"

"How do you know that?" she asked. He bent down and whispered something in her ear.

"The darling boy," she said. "Did he grow up a big boy?"

"Yes, dear Grammy," Anori said. "He became a big, strong boy."

The old lady seemed to fade away from them and settled back into her knitting, humming quietly to herself.

"We must go," Anori said.

As they left, Thordis said: "If you should see a little girl, will you tell her to come get a glass of milk."

They went back, stepping over the worshipping guards, and lugged their backpacks along the corridor. They had taken too long. The city's roosters were beginning to crow.

"We've run out of time!" Anori said. "Which way do we go?"

Obsidiana took the envelope out of her pocket and read out its inscription:

To be opened when all other paths are closed.

She broke the seal and opened the letter.

My darling daughter, by the time you open this letter some-
thing serious will have happened. Enclosed is a map showing
the way to the glade where your mother rests beneath a
weeping willow. There is a cottage in a sheltered spot with a
little spring. You will find barrels full of nuts and flour and
there are trout in the lake. If something should happen to me
and our enemies attack the palace, you are to escape there.
In your castle chamber there is a hatch leading to a room
with a spiral staircase that will take you down to a tunnel
that goes under the city. Exit through a small opening and
follow a secret path that leads to the Seven Towers. When
you arrive there . . .

Anori grew pale.

"The Seven Towers? They're on the other side of the rift! It's impossible to get across the ocean! King Dimon must have written this letter before the kingdom split into two."

He stood there with his bag on his back and felt suddenly as if all the world's woes had been stuffed into it. Soon the whole world would start to look for her, and there would be nowhere to hide. He tried to think of another plan. Where could they go? He looked at her hands—those delicate, white hands—and the bag of food, enough for just a few weeks. How were they to survive? She didn't know how to do anything; for the last two years he had relied on stealing food from the palace's half-full pantry, so he didn't really know how he would cope either.

"Let's just go. We'll find somewhere," he said.

Obsidiana stood frozen, at a loss. "My dad loves me," she whispered.

"Come on! We've no more time!"

But Obsidiana hesitated. "He'll die if I go, won't he?"

"What do you mean?"

"If I'm the one who keeps the kingdom together, then Dad will die if I leave. Isn't that right?"

Anori stamped his feet. "Dimon is crazy! He wrote this letter more than twenty years ago. You must come. You can't save him."

But she whispered, "If I leave, no sacrifices will come in and then he won't get his supplies and he will lose the war. Overthrown kings suffer a cruel fate."

"Come on, hurry!"

"But I can't let him die! I can't turn my back on him even if all the rest of the world has."

She took off her necklace and handed it to Anori. "Go find my father! Tell him to come back. The necklace is proof. I'll be waiting for you."

"No! It can't be done! I don't know where he is. I can't go alone, you don't understand how huge the world is! You're in danger! We have to leave. NOW! TOGETHER!"

Obsidiana stood facing him and tied her red scarf round his neck. He was taller than her now, but only a short while ago had been just a scruffy little boy. She straightened his hair and kissed him gently—a kiss that lasted no more than a second but to Anori felt as if it went on for a hundred thousand years.

She hurried back to her chamber and disappeared into the casket. Anori was left by himself. He swore. Goddamn king! Goddamn crazy, homicidal king! Now, he was supposed to steal a horse and go find the king, riding across moorlands and dark forests, over mountains and deserts, evading bandits and cannibals, and he would have to do all this and then persuade a crazy king to come with him before the rebels succeeded in their plot to break into the palace and kill the princess, his daughter. He had to risk his life for a man who had sacrificed his own father's life like a pawn.

He was still cursing as he crawled out of the rabbit hole to be met by a large black shadow towering over him and hands that seized him by the scruff of the neck.

The Crash

The Pangean Empire shrank—country by country, region by region, city by city. King Dimon and his men were like specters, driven from pillar to post around the remnants of his realm. Scurvy had taken all their teeth; rickets had deformed their bones; battles, infections, disease, and wild beasts had eaten away at their limbs.

They trailed along, mocked and taunted, in a grotesque file: three lame rhinos, eighteen infirm bees, fourteen frenzied archers, two blind coachmen, a caged hyena that couldn't stop laughing, a scattering of foot soldiers, one horse, and four brave knights riding together on a donkey. The men all had unwavering faith in their master; they would never betray their lord, King Dimon the Great. At the back of the line came Consiglio, limping and bent, with the Falcon of Paradise, now old and featherless as a plucked chicken. Dimon maintained his dignity and respect as best he could.

Advancing across marshy country, they had now arrived at a swamp.

"Let us cross here, comrades," said Dimon. But as he looked right he saw a crocodile dragging one of the men away.

"Whisperers, have you completely lost control of the animals?"

He looked to his left and saw a man clutching at a tree trunk, white-faced. Piranha fish had devoured him up to the waist.

Dimon felt the circumstances warranted some words of encouragement:

"Onward! Onward! The empire of Pangea will rise again!" A week later they arrived at the gates of a city. They were locked. The soldiers were hoarse and could not shout loudly enough to make themselves heard, but after a long wait a woman appeared at the gate. Consiglio waved a piece of paper.

"According to this treaty the city standing here is now part of the Pangean Empire. Open the gates and greet your king!"

Children appeared atop the battlements and began to throw dog poop at them.

Dimon yelled: "Give up! Resistance is futile!" The city gates swung open and they were ushered into a banquet hall where a fat prince sat feasting with his court; his wife flung the king a haughty glance and refused to greet him. Dimon opened his briefcase and instructed them to sign the treaty.

"I bring you the blessing of the Eternal Princess."

But the prince replied: "I've heard it said that she does not reside with the gods, but prowls around at night with the Black Prince, and is responsible for disappearances and child-snatching."

"That is not true," said Dimon. "She waits to succeed to the throne."

"I have heard also that the misfortunes suffered by the state began when the Eternal Princess first appeared in public. Even here, people have seen her roaming around at night."

"I don't know what the rats whisper in your ear when you're sitting on the john," Dimon replied, "but I can assure you that Obsidiana will come to reign over Pangea forever."

The prince grasped the hilt of his sword, but then stopped himself and said:

"I can't be bothered to kill you. Each day you live is your own defeat."

*

Soldiers surrounded Dimon and his troops, seized them, tarred and feathered them, and drove them along the main street with a herd of pigs; as the city gates slammed shut behind them, Dimon waved the treaty document and yelled:

"You haven't signed the treaty yet!" It was not mercy or a sense of pity that saved the king's life, it was because, deep inside, people feared the princess's revenge; deep inside, people believed the stories that said the world's misfortunes were her doing.

"We press on!" Dimon shouted.

"Is that a good idea?" Consiglio asked. "Let's stay in the summer palace! We can gather our strength there before we go into battle again."

The battered parade barely made it to the king's run-down summer palace before darkness. It was totally abandoned, and the men had to fight their way through a thicket of vegetation to find the main hall. As they lit lanterns against the gloom Dimon looked around. He had built this castle a long time ago, but never found time to stay in it until now.

Pieces of murals by great masters had crashed down and cracked what had been a perfectly polished marble floor. All color had faded to gray and the paintings were moldy and warped. Dimon cursed as Consiglio tried to straighten one of them.

"It's not worth fixing anything," he muttered. "Time ruins everything in the end."

He picked up ancient books that turned to dust in his hands. He ordered the oldest and most precious wines fetched from the cellar, but only red sand came trickling from the bottles. Everything he had built up or acquired had crumbled, molded, rotted, rusted, and disintegrated. No one, not even if he had a million arms-bearing men, could protect him against time.

Furtively, he gazed around; he stared fixedly into corners, mopping his sweaty brow; he peered behind the drapes, he looked up at the ceiling, he spun round as if expecting someone to sneak up behind and attack him.

"Are you there?" he whispered. "Eh? Are you there, old Father Time?"

Time was like water to him—a cold, deep water that filled all his senses so he couldn't catch his breath and felt as if his eardrums were exploding and his eyes were popping out of his head. Time was like a lion roaring at him. Time irritated him like a midge buzzing at his ear. He scratched himself as if timebugs were feasting busily on his joints, hollowing his bones, ripping his teeth out, and sucking his sight away. Time was a swarm of flies that buzzed in his head, unraveled his memories and flew away with them.

The memories of his lovely queen grew fainter as the timebugs flew away with one detail after another, one event after another. They flew away with the first touch, the first kiss, the sparkle in her eyes.

The only thing Dimon had left to hang onto was the thought of Obsidiana. Whatever else had come about, he had at least conquered time—back in the castle was a casket made of spiders' silk containing his most precious possession. Dimon felt his strength coming back, and he scribbled a few words on a note, tied it to a mail crow, and sent it off.

Dear Citizens of Pangea! Victory is just around the corner!

Hang the Thief

When Obsidiana gave Anori the necklace and kissed him goodbye, she wished from the bottom of her heart that by getting back into the casket she would be able to sail past all misfortune, skipping across the waves of time, until she arrived at a safe harbor. When the casket reopened she would see Anori and her father with smiles on their faces, and they would laugh and say: Everything is alright now. But that was not what happened. The sight that greeted her when the casket opened was Gunnhild, her face white as a sheet, holding the glittering necklace.

"Did you lose this?" said Gunnhild coldly, tossing the necklace into the casket.

"Where did you get this?" said Obsidiana. "WHERE DID YOU GET THE NECKLACE?"

In a voice of icy calm the queen replied: "A thief sneaked into the palace, can you believe it? Outrageous, but nothing is sacred in this kingdom anymore. He must have stolen the necklace from you."

Obsidiana cast around for something to hang onto, some clue as to time.

"Where is he?" she said with contempt in her eyes. "What have you done with him?"

"Done with him? Thieves aren't any of my business. They get hanged, of course."

"Where is my father? I must see him."

"What makes you think he is here? He's never around when you want him."

"I want to speak with Exel!"

"Stop this nonsense, child, and come see how thieves are hanged. Your father has obviously taught you nothing about how to govern a realm! You need to keep law and order. Now is a good time for you to behave like a real leader and oversee an execution. It's good practice. Then you might even be able to run a little war of your own."

She pushed Obsidiana ahead of her out onto the balcony. Down on the square a scaffold had been erected, onto which seven hooded men were now being led. As the executioner lifted the hoods a little in order to slip nooses around the men's necks, Obsidiana caught sight of the red scarf. She also recognized the shoes. It was Anori. She looked around, feeling sick and dizzy.

"But they mustn't be hanged," she stammered. "They can't!"

"Well now, good Princess," said Gunnhild merrily. "A farmer doesn't just bring lambs into the world; later, there's always the slaughter. You must practice. Your father didn't become king without executing people. Now, give the signal!"

"No! Stop! Stop the execution!" She was hoping for a miracle. Anori couldn't die. She looked up to the sky—if the gods existed, they had to save him.

"Give the signal!" Gunnhild ordered.

"No, you hag!"

"You want me to do it for you? You want to be your usual innocent self? Give the signal!"

"NO!!"

"Well done," Gunnhild said. "That was the signal."

The trapdoors opened and the men fell, the ropes snapping tight, and they swung jerkily to and fro; one of them kept on jiggling until a soldier approached and plunged a spear into him.

Obsidiana's eyes filled with tears; she could see nothing. Anori couldn't be dead. When he had said that the journey would be dangerous it hadn't even occurred to her that he could actually die. That he could stop living. She wished she had a casket that would take her backward in time. Then she would have gone with him carrying nothing but a bagful of food; they might have been hounded and hungry, but they would be together—and he would be alive.

The boy with the scarf hung motionless. "Excellent," said Gunnhild. "Thanks to you, justice has been served."

Obsidiana looked at her and with a frantic scowl opened her eyes wide and shouted:

"I DON'T WANT TO SEE YOU EVER AGAIN! NO ONE IS TO OPEN THE CASKET UNTIL YOU'RE ALL DEAD! I DON'T WANT TO SEE YOU!"

She ran back to the casket, jumped in, and slammed it shut. But a moment later the lid opened again, and she found herself surrounded by a cold, poisonous fog.

The Red Scarf

S crambling out of the hole, Anori was blindsided by someone grabbing the scruff of his neck.

"So that's where you are, you little shit! I knew you were
keeping something from us! What you got there?"

Anori clenched his fist around his precious keepsake, but the
man stepped on his wrist, forcing him to release his grip.

"A necklace!" the man shrieked. "Guys! It's her necklace!" He
looked furtively around. "How'd you get this?" The red-haired
man with the green eyes rummaged through Anori's bag.

"Here's enough food for days! Grains, bread, almonds, dried
fruit!" He thrust a bag full of dried fish in Anori's face.

"You know how much this stuff costs? Where'd you get this?
I haven't seen so much food since back in the good times."

Anori said nothing. "This is the hole where we lost you all that
time ago! You told us you didn't find anything," said the first one.

"Hey, look at that!" the red-haired guy said. "The scarf has the
princess's crest on it!" He snatched the red scarf from around
Anori's neck. "And look at his shoes! Even high society dudes
don't have fancy shoes like these."

"I trusted you," he said, looking straight into Anori's eyes. "We
were supposed to go together. You betrayed me!"

Anori looked away. The redhead tied the scarf round his neck
and removed Anori's shoes, while the rest of the gang interro-
gated the boy.

"Where'd you get this stuff?" The man kicked him. "What were you up to? What's in there?"

They bound his arms and legs and sat him up. "Is that witch with the frown in there?"

Anori didn't answer.

"You in league with the court? Are you taking bribes from the guy who killed your father?"

The man twisted his finger. "There's nothing in there!" Anori howled with pain.

But Anori knew it was no use lying. They would soon find the way up the tower and through the hatch to the room where Obsidiana lay defenseless. The men gagged him. He squirmed against his bonds but could only watch as they disappeared one by one into the hole. They would find her and kill her. The last thing Anori was aware of was a club raised over him that suddenly swung down and turned everything black.

Dimon Comes to His Senses

D imon was outside the Summer Palace giving first aid to a sick rhino when a bedraggled crow landed nearby, strolled toward him, bowed, and extended a leg. The king untied the note:

> *System failure at the palace; strengths are minimal, threats many, opportunities few. The corners of the princess's mouth are turned down, indicating unhappiness. Urchin and Gunnhild are turning your allies against you. Results of my calculations indicate they would like you dead.*
>
> > *Certified and logged – Exel*

The king scratched his head. Consiglio brought a morsel of meat, which the crow devoured. A short while later, another crow arrived; this one had a capsule attached to its leg.

> *Go back to the pass.*
> *According to my calculations, all other routes are blocked.*
> *The capsule contains a substance that will render you invincible.*
>
> > *Best wishes – Exel*

"Back to the pass?" he snorted. "Back to where we were show-ered with arrows and burning tar?" He held the message up to the sunlight and saw that it was written on lined paper. Exel would never write on lined paper. Dimon picked up the magic capsule with two fingers and scrutinized the gray-green powder it contained. Seeing a squirrel running up and down a nearby tree, Dimon poured the powder onto a stone; the squirrel came and licked at it, and immediately began to behave strangely. Its pupils contracted, and it bared its teeth before bolting up the tallest tree, where it sat cockily, not noticing the owl that glided silently over, dug its claws into it and flew off with it.

Poison, Dimon thought. Somebody wanted him dead. "Consiglio," he said, "What day is it today?"

"Do you want a real answer or an easy one?"

"A real answer."

"Wednesday."

"What month?"

"Spring month."

"What year?"

"According to which calendar?"

"The new one."

"It hasn't started yet."

"The old one, then!"

"It's forty years since the battle of Hill Top."

"That's impossible," Dimon said. "That means I'm seventy years old." He rubbed the dust and grime from his shield, and in its reflection saw an old, toothless man with only one eye and a nose that looked as if it had been stitched onto his face. He had lost three fingers, two toes, half an ear, a kidney, and most of his hair.

"I conquered the world, then lost it again, but I did succeed in conquering time," he said. "If something happens to Obsidiana then I have lost everything!"

Dimon surveyed his wretched troop, and then, leaping astride the one remaining horse, cried: "I'm off to the palace!"

The horse snorted, reared, and then galloped off at such speed that the king had to hang on for dear life. As he thus abandoned what was left of his army, Dimon shouted: "Giddyup! Giddyup, my beauty! To the palace!"

The Red Panda

Anori regained consciousness to find himself bound and gagged, his hands tied behind his back, and unable to move. He could see the little hole the gang had disappeared into but couldn't tell if the men had re-emerged yet. It was only a moment ago that Obsidiana had kissed him, just before everything went black. They must be in there with her now, and he knew what they meant to do.

He shifted around, trying to bite through the gag. He realized that it was not out of sympathy that they had held back from cutting his throat right away—it was far worse for him to die of heat and thirst out here in the open. He writhed around and saw that one of his hands was going blue from lack of blood. Ants crawled into his ears and the corners of his eyes, and he winced when they bit him; they obviously intended to take him in tiny bits back to their anthill.

But then an animal appeared, one that he recognized from pictures in the palace. It was the ancient red panda, lazily snuffling around in the garbage in the alleyway. It came up to him, sniffed, and began to pick the ants off him, putting them in its mouth and crushing them with a faint snap between its teeth. Anori murmured and turned over on his side to show the panda the rope, but it backed off and disappeared.

215

"Don't go!" Anori mumbled through the gag. The panda soon reappeared, this time clutching a rat in its paws—a one-eyed rat, ragged and gray with a long tail. The panda released it, and it scurried toward Anori, whose eyes dilated with fear as the animal sniffed his nose, scrabbled across his face, and darted down the neck of his shirt and out again through a sleeve. The panda recaptured it and pressed it up against the rope, and the rat began gnawing; it gnawed uncomfortably close to Anori's skin, but he tugged and strained until he was able to snap the rope. He rubbed his hands together to get the blood flow going again, while the panda lumbered around him. He looked at the hole in the wall and couldn't bear the thought that the gang would probably have completed its mission by now. He retrieved his bow and arrows and crawled through the hole, but hadn't gone far into the darkness of the castle when he heard guards talking:

"Any more here?"

"I found where they got in!"

Anori saw the flicker of their torches. He crawled quickly back, intending to escape onto the street, but spied the panda on the roof above him. He hauled himself up onto a window ledge and followed the animal to a little hidey-hole, where they waited a while as the guards ran around looking for more intruders. Then the panda darted off toward the castle's outer wall, towering above the cliffs, and began to clamber skillfully up the branches of the thorn trees that clung to it. Anori followed, ignoring the thorns digging deep into the palms of his hands. He looked down to where waves crashed onto the ragged rocks at the foot of the cliffs far below him, but then, directing his gaze resolutely upward, he climbed higher, inching along and at times having to swing to regain a handhold when the thorn branches came away from the wall and left him dangling by one hand. The panda was waiting for him by a window as Anori heaved himself up onto the narrow walkway for archers that stretched along the full length of the battlements. In the room below, Anori spotted the casket and heaved a sigh of relief; not knowing if it was yet safe to approach it, he crouched down alongside the panda and waited patiently. Through an opening, he saw the seven figures hanging from the gallows down on the square. Despite their hoods, he recognized them immediately, and he could see Obsidiana's red scarf flapping in the breeze. There had been times when he wished those guys dead, but now the situation was different. He thought about the woman at the inn, the soup with the chunks of meat, and the men sitting by the fireside. He felt his stomach drop. These were the men who had hoped to overthrow Dimon and make the world better. He had promised them he would avenge his father's death, and he had betrayed them.

At the city's outermost limit a man was seen approaching on horseback, his mount drenched in sweat. King Dimon was on his way home.

Anori Under the Rafters

Anori was in the process of climbing down into Obsidiana's chamber when Urchin came clanking into the room, accompanied by Gunnhild. Anori tried to make himself invisible. He drew his bow and waited, poised to shoot. Anybody wanting to harm Obsidiana would find themselves on the sharp end of an arrow.

Urchin walked over to the casket and scratched at the lid. "Look how beautiful she is," he said, "even when she is sad."

"What are you planning, Urchin? Why have you brought me here?"

"Dimon is done for," he said. "I have heard he is on his way home. When they can be bothered, his enemies will crush him."

"What do you want to do?"

Urchin stared at the casket and the beautiful girl inside it. His eyes gleamed as he pulled out a sharp knife. "Plunge a knife into her heart," he said, "and your daughters will inherit the kingdom."

Gunnhild took a step back and gave him an ice-cold look.

"That's what you desire, isn't it?" Urchin went on. "You've wanted to get rid of her for a long time. You hate her. She is never pleased with you and she bad-mouths you to the gods."

He offered her the knife. Gunnhild looked at this scrawny man with his golden chains and his ridiculous robe.

"What's in it for you?" she asked. "My daughters are not your daughters."

"We could reign together," Urchin said, unctuously.

"That would never work."

"Of course it would."

"No, because I know what you're thinking. You want to get rid of Dimon and me as well. You want to possess the Eternal Princess."

Urchin looked at her with hate in his eyes and rattled his chains. All at once he thrust the knife into Gunnhild's hand, turned, and tore open the lid of the casket, yelling:

"Look out, Obsidiana! Gunnhild is going to kill you! Guards! Gunnhild is trying to stab the princess!"

Time, cruel and merciless time, seeped in and engulfed Obsidiana like a cold, poisonous fog. Gunnhild had forced her to oversee the execution of her one and only friend; she had seen Anori swinging from the scaffold and wanted most of all never to see anything ever again. But now here was Urchin standing over the casket looking savage and bellowing:

"GUARDS! Gunnhild is going to stab Obsidiana!" Gunnhild stood dumbfounded, holding the knife.

The door burst open and King Dimon roared: "Who opened the casket? Who is wasting my daughter's precious time?" He drew his bow, aimed straight for Urchin, and let fly an arrow.

Meanwhile, up in the rafters, Anori, determined to use his only arrow to save the princess, had been following Urchin's movements. Anori kept his arrow trained on him as he darted toward the casket and ripped it open, but Urchin's warning shouts drew Anori's attention to Gunnhild, standing beside the casket holding a knife. Yelling, "WATCH OUT, OBSIDIANA!" he swiftly took aim at the queen and fired.

Two arrows crisscrossed the chamber, one heading straight for Urchin, the other for Gunnhild. Obsidiana lay, eyes closed, in the casket when she heard familiar voices.

"Father? Anori?" she whispered in surprise. Opening her eyes wide, she sat bolt upright.

Obsidiana looked round to see Gunnhild turn, quick as a flash, and sink the knife into Urchin's heart. She looked up to where Anori's voice had come from and found herself gazing straight into his eyes; there he was, sitting under the rafters with his unkempt hair and his gentle eyes. Her heart missed a beat and she felt as if it had been struck by an arrow. Which was, in fact, precisely what had happened. An arrow pierced her heart at the same moment as another zinged through Gunnhild and out the window. Gunnhild fell on top of Urchin, and Obsidiana fell back into the casket as the lid snapped shut with a bang. It all happened so fast that she still had a light in her eyes and the blissful thought in her head: Anori is alive!

Anori had watched the arrow cleave the air and saw Obsidiana start up; he looked straight into her eyes before she flinched and he saw that an arrow had plunged deep into her chest. His heart shrank like a star collapsing under its own weight and turned into a black hole.

The king saw Gunnhild fall and Urchin collapse and his daughter disappear back into the casket. He ran in panic into the chamber. The queen lay in a pool of blood, Urchin by her side with the knife in his heart. And the beautiful Princess, his great treasure, lay in her magic casket. He heaved a sigh of relief and was about to fling the lid open and embrace her after all this time when he was horror-struck to see the arrow.

There were only three drops of blood in the casket. Obsidiana was not dead, but he realized that, were he to open the casket, her life would seep away and dissolve in a moment. Like the Albino Flower.

The Black Prince

When Anori slowly came to his senses, he found himself wandering amid servants and palace guards running hither and thither in chaos and confusion. He didn't care if they hanged him. From the chamber came the sound of King Dimon howling in grief.

"The king shot her," the servants wailed.

"The king shot her!" the guards yelled. "Urchin and Gunnhild were going to kill her. It's terrible!"

Wasn't it me who shot her? Anori thought. He drifted trance-like through the palace as guards and ladies-in-waiting rushed around weeping, bumping into him and shouting:

"Out of the way! Out of the way! We have to do something!" But nobody knew what that something was, and nobody thought of arresting him. Anori was fighting back tears. Whoever had fired that arrow, it was now buried deep in the princess's heart. Her very last moment was preserved in the casket for all eternity—she was not dead, but neither was she alive. There had to be something he could do.

Anori felt a warm hand grasp his. "Dear, dear, my little one. Are you sad? What happened?" Anori looked round. It was Thordis. She led Anori along the corridor, past bewildered guards and weeping maids. The castle gates were open, and they heard the sound of horses' hooves as Goldwillow and Silverwillow fled the castle in panic.

Anori and Thordis walked slowly through the city. He was dazzled by the sunlight as Thordis led him along streets that she seemed to know like the back of her hand.

"Well, well, I never! Has the corner store closed?" she exclaimed in surprise as they walked past an abandoned house. She made straight for the home of Anori's aunt.

"My dear Borghild," she said, "I'm sorry I'm so late. I seem to have forgotten to buy the bread."

For a moment Borghild stared at her sister in disbelief, and then they fell into one another's arms.

While they were embracing, Anori stared up at the ceiling, where a spider sat in one corner. He caught it and put it in a small bottle, and then fetched a stick and spun its web into a ball.

At the palace, Dimon stood pale as death. Consiglio arrived on horseback with the remnants of the army.

"Consiglio! Somebody must be able to save her," Dimon said.

Consiglio looked through the lid of the casket, at the lovely girl with the arrow in her heart. His eyes filled with pain as if all his bees had stung him at once.

"You know full well that a wound in the heart is fatal."

"No!" said the king. "We have time, somebody in this world must be able to save her."

Consiglio shook his head. "You know the saying: 'There's no point dressing a fatal wound.' The moment you open the casket she will bleed to death. No doctor exists who is quick enough to save her. All you can do is open the casket and tell her that you love her."

Dimon thundered: "Whoever can save Obsidiana's life will be rewarded with half the kingdom!"

223

"What kingdom?" said Consiglio. "There's nothing left of the kingdom."

"As soon as I have reconquered my kingdom that person will get half of it. Send out an order to the best doctors and most skillful craftsmen! Find the dwarfs!"

"But you had them beheaded, Sire," said Consiglio, shaking his head.

The castle gates were locked and every door was bolted. At night, the palace was in utter darkness save for a faint light up in a turret where Dimon sat waiting for someone to come who could fix an incurable heart wound. Years passed and the king waited, but nobody stepped forward.

Up in the mountains there were rumors of a mysterious figure traveling around—a black-clad man astride a horse trailing a wagon. Other travelers ran away on his approach, whispering:

"It's the Black Prince!" Villagers locked their shutters as the wagon rattled past, laden with jars full of spiders. Two gray-haired old women with spinning wheels sat on the wagon bed spinning thread.

At regular intervals Anori stopped to scan the surrounding forest. If he spotted a big spider's web he would poke a long stick into it, twirling it like cotton candy, and then hand it over to one of his companions for her to separate the web and spin it into thread. The women looked happy and were extremely productive.

"Well, Thordis, dear sister, we finally got to go traveling together!"

"Traveling?" Thordis said, continuing to spin. "Are we traveling?"

Anori stopped the wagon at the mouth of a cave and unloaded the balls of silk and the spider jars. Inside the cave he created a living space and set up a loom. He was soon weaving the yarn the old women had spun. He picked and battened, picked and battened, picked and battened, all through that fall and the following winter. When the spring sun shone in through the mouth of the cave he stopped to inspect the fruits of his labor, holding up to the light a small piece of spider silk that looked like an extremely thin icicle. He looked at the fabric and shed a tear, while the old women lay snoring in their beds.

A small creature approached from the innermost darkness of the cave, carrying a dim lantern that cast a long and slender beam of light toward him.

"I've been watching you," said a voice in the dark. "Your method of work is hopeless. It would take you ten thousand years to weave a whole casket."

The creature came closer, and Anori saw it was an aged dwarf-woman.

"I have to press on," he said.

"Nobody can draw an arrow from a heart wound."

"I know," said Anori. "I'm going to weave a casket and send myself forward in time. It's the only way I can see her again."

"You shouldn't keep running after the Eternal Princess. Her fate is a warning to all."

"She didn't do anything wrong; she just wanted to experience time like everyone else."

The dwarf woman considered this. "This is what happens when people seek vengeance," she muttered, gazing at Anori with her enormous eyes.

"I wasn't seeking vengeance."

"Revenge always hurts the one who least deserves it. The casket was a revenge gift from my brothers."

"Please let me work," Anori said. "I have no time to lose."

"I can't go on watching you weave so badly; you're a disgrace to the profession. The spiders you have are totally useless, and you're stroking them the wrong way."

She led Anori farther into the recesses of the cave. When his eyes had gotten used to the dark he saw five dwarfs with large, hairy spiders on their laps; they stroked them gently as if they were cats, and pulled long silvery threads out of them.

The old woman pondered.

"Who knows, maybe we could give you a little help."

The Angry Mob

It was morning, and an angry mob had gathered outside the royal palace. Dimon, wandering listlessly around, watched from the window of his ceremonial hall as the throng demolished the temple, invaded the palace gardens, and started smashing statues. He hardly reacted at all to this spectacle, not even when his guards were overpowered and disarmed. The mob surrounded the palace and a group of citizens set about forcing the drawbridge open.

"Time! Accursed time!" muttered Dimon, shaking his head. To him this screaming horde was no different from time, which for all these years had been crumbling the fabric of the palace; it was just that the people were bigger than the timebugs.

Consiglio approached. He had stowed his bees into a small box.

"It's all over, Your Majesty," he said. "The people will break in here any moment. We must escape through the secret passage."

The king ignored him.

"Dimon, you have to bid her farewell." He pointed at the casket, where Obsidiana lay in her timeless beauty—wearing a white dress, radiant with joy, but with an arrow in her heart.

"The mob will be here any moment. You must take her in your arms and say goodbye. She is your daughter, after all."

"No," said the king. "She is not dead, and thanks to the casket she never has to die."

"Preserving her last moment for eternity is futile," said Consiglio firmly. "If I were king, I would order you to open it and take leave of her."

"No. There is always hope."

A shower of rocks shattered the windows, but the king scarcely moved a muscle as the stones landed at his feet. The tumult outside grew louder, and now the mob was pushing at the great oak doors leading into the hall. As they crashed through the doors, Consiglio stabbed the leading intruder with his sword, but was immediately trampled to death by the flood of people that engulfed him: vagrants, soldiers, deserters, old women, youngsters, farmers—a rabid, leaderless mob. There was a momentary silence as the people stopped and gazed around the hall, into which the public had never been allowed. They stared in disbelief at the bearded man sitting on the throne. Dimon was silent, immobile. He looked a little surprised when the mob surged toward him and the man at the front raised his ax to strike him. The king looked up at the vaulted ceiling and the painting that showed him standing in all his glory with the world in his hand. Suddenly something whistled toward him and the world inside his head exploded as he fell to the floor. From the corner of his eye he saw the casket, and then his sight filled with white light and gentle, eternal darkness. A woman tore down one of the thick drapes, and the morning sun burst into the hall, bathing it in brightness. A shaft of sunlight shone on the girl lying motionless in the casket, illuminating her wondrous beauty and radiant countenance. The man who had chopped down the king and was now poised to strike the princess stood as if frozen, and then slowly lowered his weapon to the floor. No one dared utter a word; no one dared approach the casket. The sun shone on the black hair, the blood-red lips, the pale cheeks, and the arrow in her heart. Then it was as if a herd of reindeer was stampeding: someone turned and ran, and the rest of the mob followed, terrified of the fatal curse that almost certainly accompanied this fearful girl.

Obsidiana had no idea that all she knew and loved was completely gone; her expression remained unchanged until a black-clad man opened the casket very briefly and put a note in her hand, whispering softly: "We will meet again!"

Obsidiana gasped, her chest turned bright red, and she moved another moment closer to death.

Days passed, seasons, years. Time demolished the castle with the force of a hundred thousand flowers that spread and flourished in every chink and cranny, proving more powerful than the mightiest king that ever reigned on Earth. Their seeds settled on the king and sent roots through his belly and chest, drawing their nourishment from his body. Two small green buds sprouted from his eye sockets and became two young shoots that reached out for the sun and twined and twisted around each other like a narwhal's tooth; they grew into a twisted tree, which forced its way through the roof, spreading a green canopy over the princess and wrapping its roots in a firm embrace around the casket, which over countless centuries gradually disappeared beneath the forest floor.

Here the princess lay, timeless and eternal, neither alive nor dead, millennia old and yet only fourteen.

A Story Ends

Grace finished speaking.

"And then what?"

"That's how the story of Pangea ends," she said.

"No, it can't end like that," said Marcus.

Grace looked serious. "I'm sorry, but the truth is that if you all do nothing you will suffer the same fate as Obsidiana."

"What do you mean?"

"For years I have watched as thistles and briars have blanketed the world. It won't be long now before the houses finally collapse and the city disappears beneath the forest floor; when that happens it will be too late for people in the time caskets to re-emerge into the world."

The children sat transfixed by her words. Sigrun imagined a world overrun by forests populated with birds and deer, while the human race remained frozen underground like ancient mammoths. A great earthquake might break open the caskets so that people would wake up in moss-encrusted rooms deep down in the earth. Those who could manage to find their way to the surface would roam around, scared and confused, their only hope to crawl back into their caskets.

"What can we do?" Marcus asked.

"The curse of the princess of Pangea spread throughout the world because someone found her casket and worked out how to

230

mass-produce it. Only someone else who understands the origins of the curse can turn the world around and make it better. I have a sequel to read to you."

She fetched another bundle of papers.

Hidden Treasure

They had driven for several hours alongside the rocky shore when at last a small, humble village came into view, snuggled in a dell beneath a tree-covered hill. Its houses were ancient and falling apart; the world seemed to have forgotten this place. Archaeologists James Cromwell and Victor Rowland stopped at a dilapidated café. They were dusty, sweaty, and filthy from the dirt roads they had traveled.

An old man hobbled out and addressed them in a language they didn't understand, which their guide translated for them: "What are you doing here?"

"Just looking around," Cromwell replied.

"There's nothing here to see," the man snapped.

"In that case, we'll just take a walk," said Cromwell, pointing at the tree-covered hill overlooking the village.

"You must not go anywhere near the Forbidden Hill! It's cursed and nobody has gone there for thousands of years!"

The hair bristled on the back of Rowland's neck, but Cromwell listened intently; in the past, folk stories had often been of assistance in his search for valuable remains.

Early the following morning a black helicopter landed in a forest glade on the far side of the hill. The pilot seemed agitated as he stopped the rotor: "I'll wait, but I'm not making any promises. If anything unexpected happens up there, I'm out of here!"

The village below was hidden in mist, and the morning dew soaked Cromwell's and Rowland's feet as they dropped to the ground. They trod gingerly as if navigating a minefield, and jumped when crows came flying from a nearby tree and circled vulture-like around them. The stories they'd heard had affected their nerves.

It was obvious the area had been inhabited a very long time ago. As they cleared away the vegetation, the outlines of solid stone walls came into view.

"Incredible," said Rowland, moving his metal detector slowly over the ground and hearing beeps from it with every other step he took.

Cromwell was beside himself with excitement—even a tin can from this era would make him a millionaire.

"It's as if people fled from here in panic." Cromwell fetched his tools, removed a sod of turf, and began scraping the earth away. He hadn't removed much soil before uncovering a golden bowl and a coin; using his water bottle to wash the dirt off the coin, he revealed the profile of a king and an inscription in a language he was not familiar with.

"I've never seen anything like this," he said. "This is real treasure! No one has been here for thousands of years. Those dumb villagers would be millionaires if they weren't so obsessed with that curse."

As he pocketed the gold coin, his eyes were drawn to a peculiarly twisted oak tree that dominated the hill. It had two trunks intertwined like a gigantic narwhal's tooth, and looked ancient, its bark gray as the skin of an age-old tortoise. The wind whistled eerily in its leaves as if telling them to run away to safety, but from its more delicate branches came a gentler whisper that drew them toward it.

Rowland felt beads of sweat on his forehead as he warily circled the tree with his metal detector. Its beeping grew louder as he moved closer to the trunk, until there was a sudden terrible screech and its screen died. He looked up and it seemed as if there were faces embedded in the bark.

"Useless piece of junk!" said Rowland, his voice faltering. Cromwell kept his distance as Rowland struggled to reset the detector, and covered his ears when the detector screeched again and stopped working at exactly the same spot.

"There's something down here," Rowland said, "something that's overloading the detector."

Cromwell began to dig enthusiastically.

"That's not exactly in the spirit of good archaeology," Rowland said. "Digging like that you'll destroy valuable evidence."

"We'll never excavate this site with one of your teaspoons," Cromwell said, "and if we don't hurry, we'll never get out of here."

They had reached a depth of about ten feet when the spade broke.

"Here's something!" said Rowland excitedly, wiping the sweat off his brow with a sleeve. "But we must hurry, the sun is setting."

Cromwell joined him in the hole they had dug. "It's some kind of casket," said Rowland. It was covered with moss, and the oak clutched it greedily with thick, finger-like roots. The two men began sawing at the wood to free the thing, but the tree was reluctant to give up its precious possession; as soon as one root broke, another seemed to twist itself around the casket like a snake. They kept on cutting, even using a blowtorch to burn through the roots, and then suddenly it was as if the tree released its grip, and its canopy of branches creaked miserably as the pair looped a rope under the casket and heaved it out of the hole.

They could see a line of torches down in the village slowly making their way toward the hill.

In the distance they heard the helicopter starting up. "Quick, before he leaves us behind!" They dragged the casket through the trees as fast as they could, hauled it aboard the helicopter, and moments later were flying away above the wood.

"We'd probably be dead by now," said Rowland, looking down at the torch lights congregating where the helicopter had been only moments before.

They flew back, following the long, rocky coastline, and watched the sun sink below the horizon. Cromwell and Rowland breathed more easily now, their nervous laughter all but drowned out by the noise of the helicopter. After a two-hour flight they landed at a large ranch on the outskirts of a city and carried the casket into a nearby outbuilding, where they scraped off bits of moss and earth and cut away the remaining roots wrapped around it. Their hearts skipped a beat when they detected the faint outlines of a human inside it. Cromwell felt around the lid until he found the catch.

"Be careful opening it," said Rowland. With a sucking noise, the casket opened and time flooded into it like water filling a sinking ship. Then they heard a heavy moan.

"Oh my God!" said Cromwell, and flung the lid wide open. Inside lay a girl with an arrow through her heart. She opened her eyes and her dress was instantly drenched with blood; she gasped and coughed, and blood trickled from the corners of her mouth.

"She's wounded!" Cromwell took her in his arms and ran toward the helicopter. "Quick! Quick! GET IN THE CHOPPER! She has an arrow in her heart! HURRY!"

The pilot, who'd been sitting in the yard, half-choked on his coffee and sprinted to the helicopter. He quickly got the blades going as Rowland jumped aboard, closely followed by Cromwell, carrying the girl and yelling:

"Let's go! Let's go!"

The helicopter took off into the darkness and sped over the bright lights of the city. They pressed the wound tightly, trying to stop the bleeding, while the girl stared up at the cabin roof, coughing and finally losing consciousness. Her face was as white as snow; her hair was as black as a raven's wing; her dress was as red as blood.

"Faster!" shouted Rowland. "Call the hospital and tell them we're on our way!"

Soon they saw the brightly lit bulk of the hospital, towering twenty stories high over the neighboring suburbs. The chopper thumped down heavily onto the helipad, and white-coated orderlies tore open the door, heaved the girl onto a gurney, and raced off through swing doors into the building.

Cromwell and Rowland were left behind, silent, covered with dirt and blood. Rowland was crying. Far below they could hear the hum of traffic and the hustle and bustle of the city. The air felt polluted and muggy.

"Those villagers are crazy," Cromwell said. "They must have buried her alive."

"But how? How could they have done that? We had to cut through roots to get at the casket."

Cromwell thought. "I don't understand it. It didn't look like there'd been any digging there before us. The villagers are concealing something. They must practice human sacrifice on that hill. I've never known anything like it! To bury a girl alive!"

They waited at the hospital all night. Police came to question them.

Cromwell was upset: "She was shot by some crazy villagers!"

"Where?"

"On the Forbidden Hill."

The cop shook his head. "You went there? You must be nuts! A whole team of scientists disappeared there last year. We can't get a single word outta those villagers."

In the morning, a doctor came to see them.

"It's critical. Her heart had stopped beating when she got here. We'll have to wait and see." He handed Cromwell a box. "Here are her belongings: her dress, a necklace, and a note she was clutching."

Cromwell stood there holding the box, at a loss what to do; he studied the note and recognized neither the script nor the language.

Grace set her papers aside. The children looked at her.

"You'll have to find Cromwell if you want to know more," she said. "He's the guy who appeared one day on our television screens selling TimeBoxes® to the whole world. I'm sure he knows how the story ends."

Looking for Cromwell

The NO MORE FEBRUARYS! sign flickered in the distance. Grace spread a street map on the coffee table and drew a red circle around a property in an affluent area of the city.

Marcus looked at the map. "He's living here in the city? Why didn't you say so right away?"

"Let's go find him!"

"Yes, you all know how to break windows, right?" said Grace.

Marcus blushed.

"Is he dangerous?" Peter asked.

Grace didn't answer this question. Instead, she said, "Be careful. You never know what people like him may do. Ask him about three things: the princess, Anori, and the key to the factory."

"The key to the factory?"

"Yes, I believe it's the key to lifting the spell from the world."

Marcus shook his head, but then he thought about his parents and his little sister. He had to rescue them before they disappeared underground. There was no choice; they had to do as Grace said. The children took the map and headed off; they walked along a moss-covered freeway, past the shopping mall, past the lake with the Ferris wheel, and past the building inside which a frozen line of senators stood. Sigrun looked at her neighborhood with deep sadness. She longed to go home.

They finally arrived at a district where the yards were the size of soccer fields and tired-looking stone lions stood guard over driveways.

"I wouldn't like to deliver mail in this precinct," Peter said. Cromwell's house was surrounded by high walls and thorn hedges. Near the entrance was a fountain and next to it a rusty Rolls-Royce, its tires flat and its roof coated with bird droppings. The front door of the house was locked, and the doorknob fell off when Peter tried to turn it. They walked around the back of the house, where there was a swimming pool full of leaves and a tennis court that looked like a jungle. They found a broken window, cleared away the shards of glass, and crawled in. There was no sign of life.

"Do you trust her?" Sigrun whispered.

"Grace?" Marcus shrugged. "I don't know."

Their footsteps echoed on the marble floor as they wandered around the high-ceilinged rooms. Wagtails fluttered along the corridors; a crystal chandelier lay in pieces on the floor; in the bathroom, ants were busily taking apart a dead raccoon. They climbed the staircase to the upper floor, but stopped dead on spotting a blue glow seeping out from under a door.

"Anyone fancy going in?" Marcus asked.

"Not me," said Sigrun.

"After you," said Peter.

"We'll go in together," said Kristin. Ever so slowly they pushed the door open, and found themselves in a dusty library, where stuffed animal heads stared at them out of the semidarkness and a twisted narwhal's tooth hung from the ceiling. The blue glow came from a black box standing in the corner of the room, and they jumped when they saw it contained a pale, thin man staring open-mouthed into space.

"Is this him?" said Marcus, studying the pallid, gray face.

"Ask him," Sigrun said. She hid behind Peter as Marcus, hands sweating, took out the Allen wrench and opened the box.

"Who's there? Eh? Who's there?" The man peered into the half-light of the room.

"We're looking for Mr. Cromwell."

"That's me. What are you doing here? It's wrong to open other people's boxes! STAFF! Some young hooligans have gotten in!"

"There's no staff left here," Marcus said.

"What the hell!"

"Did you make the black boxes?"

"Yes, I sure did."

"Thanks to you, then, the world's in ruins."

"Thanks to me? I didn't force people to buy them."

"But you invented the slogan 'No More Februarys.'"

"And why not? February's a lousy month."

"My birthday's in February, actually," said Sigrun, mortally offended.

"Unfortunate timing like that is no fault of mine," Cromwell snorted. He looked out the window and seemed to flinch at what he saw. He sniffed the air, frowning at the smell of mold, and tried to shake off the chilling sense of desolation. "Ugh, this situation is horrible. Well, goodbye, I have no time to lose. I'm accumulating interest. Away with you."

"No, you must help us."

"Help you?"

"We have to release the people," Sigrun said, "before it's too late."

"Folks set their own exit times. I'm not stopping anybody from coming out!"

"But they can't do that—everyone's waiting for better times to come. Nobody wants to take the initiative."

"And that's my fault? Am I supposed to spend my time clearing up the mess others leave behind? No way! Do you know how much interest I'm losing just by standing here talking to you?" He looked at the clock. "At least four hundred thousand points!"

"No one's paying interest anymore," said Marcus. Cromwell shut himself in. Marcus opened the box up again.

Cromwell peered at him. "You haven't gone, then?" Cromwell asked.

"No," said Marcus.

"Get lost!" said Cromwell, shutting the lid.

Marcus opened the box again. "We need the key."

"The key?"

"Yes."

"What key?"

"The key to the factory."

Cromwell frowned. "You're in deep water if you're after the key to the factory! Who sent you?"

"A woman named Grace."

Cromwell was stunned; he looked frightened. "Grace? Is she here with you?"

"No."

He seemed somewhat relieved. "Do not believe a word that woman says."

"Why not?"

"She's crazy. She has time caskets on the brain. She was dead against them and said I would bring the world to ruin by setting us free from time. Keep away from her! She brings nothing but treachery, tragedy, and death." He slammed the box shut. Sigrun and Marcus looked at one another and opened it yet again.

"What?"

"She let us out of our boxes so she could tell us a story."

"And we need to ask you how that story ends."

"I don't know any stories!"

"It was a story about a princess whose heart was pierced by an arrow and who was buried in a magic casket beneath the weight of time."

Cromwell thought for a moment, and then stepped out of the box. He wore tennis shoes, a pink polo shirt, and white shorts. He strolled directly over to a dirty window and, seeing the wreck of his Rolls-Royce out on the driveway, pulled a wry face.

"I'd have put it inside if I'd known how long this was going to take."

He went back to his box, checked the time switch and rapped it in disbelief.

"Wow! That was a moment and a half," he said. "The situation hasn't gotten any better?"

"No," said the kids.

"The boxes were very carefully set up. They were to open automatically as soon as the crisis was over. I just didn't expect it to last such a long time." Cromwell looked around at the warped floorboards and rotten walls and muttered: "There sure is a lot that needs to be cleaned up here."

He picked up a pair of binoculars and focused them on a factory in the distance, its red-and-white towers silhouetted against the sky. "Grace sent you to get the key?"

"Yes."

"Typical of her to try to ruin things for me."

"Do you know what happened to Obsidiana?" Sigrun asked.

"No, the name means nothing to me."

"Obsidiana was a princess who had a magic casket."

"Did she indeed. I am a businessman, I know nothing about fairy tales. Next question?"

"What happened to Anori?"

The question seemed to surprise him. "I don't know anybody called Anori. Who's he?"

"Anori was a boy who loved the princess. He wove a casket to take him into the future so they could be together again."

Cromwell's eyes widened. "There's another casket?" He reddened, realizing he had said too much.

"So, you seem to know of at least one, then," Sigrun said. Cromwell didn't reply.

"Tell us what became of the girl."

The Casket Found

Cromwell paced the floor of the library. It was hard to gauge his mood, but something seemed to be bothering him.

"Take a seat," he said.

The children sat down on the plush sofas, sending up a swirling cloud of dust. A blue-eyed antelope's head stared at them. Still pacing pensively back and forth, Cromwell heaved a sigh and began.

"The girl was kept in a coma for forty days. I visited every day. She looked extremely beautiful and peaceful as she lay there asleep, but no one knew where she came from nor what her name was. When she woke we tried to talk to her. She didn't seem to understand what we were saying, but then I remembered the note written in a strange script that she had been clutching when we found her. I handed it to her and she burst into tears. The following day she disappeared; nobody knew what had happened to her. Hardly a day went by without my thinking about her.

"It wasn't until many years later when I was working late at the lab that she suddenly appeared before me, looking like a ghost—her hair as black as night, her face as white as snow. She handed me a note in my own language and then she disappeared.

'If you take a two-day journey from the Forbidden Hill you will find a cone-shaped mountain. A river winds along the

bottom of the valley. A battle was once fought on level ground here near a pass. Look there and see what you can find.'

"I called Rowland and we headed off to the place right away, as if some magnetic force was drawing us there. We followed her instructions and found a huge cache of weapons, helmets, and valuables. There were human skeletons, and bones from elephants, horses, and rhinos. Halfway through our dig the girl appeared again. I greeted her and called out, 'Look at all this gold!' She scrutinized everything we'd found but didn't seem to be at all interested in the gold. She kept to herself, and nobody knew what her name was or where she came from. Our assistants were frightened of her. She examined the skulls carefully and read every inscription we had found. When we had finished our excavation she seemed to be deeply disappointed. She sat down on the shore and gazed out across the sea. I went and sat beside her.

"'You're looking for something.'

"'Yes,' she said, in a very thick accent.

"'Something more valuable than gold.'

"'Yes,' she said. 'You have to keep looking. You must cross the Great Rift.'

"'The Great Rift?'

"'Follow your nose, you'll find the Seven Towers,' she said, pointing to the horizon.

"'Follow my nose? Africa's twenty-five hundred miles away! But I'll go there if you tell me who you are.'

"'My name is Grace.'

"We did as she said and found the Seven Towers. Again she turned up halfway through the dig, but even though we were discovering priceless masks, statues, and remains, she shook her head and said: 'No, it's not here, it must be somewhere else.'"

"Did she know you had the casket?"

"She said I should dump it in the sea. I did promise to do that, but the thing fascinated me, and I built a state-of-the-art laboratory in my basement hoping to discover what it was made of."

The stuffed antelope's head seemed to prick up its ears.

Cromwell continued: "One day a noise woke me up. It sounded like someone had broken into the basement and was trashing the place. I ran down there and found her, eyes blazing, smashing my test tubes and microscopes and hammering at the casket with her fists. She grabbed the narwhal's tooth and thrust its sharp point at my chest, hissing at me: 'To understand a casket like this requires great wisdom, otherwise it will bring nothing but death and damnation! Those who conquer time will lose the world.' Then she hit me hard on the head. When I woke up, she was gone, and I never saw her again.

"But her words stuck in my head. Conquer time? That had never occurred to me. I realized the magic power of the casket and understood what a fantastic discovery this could be for the human race. It took me some time to develop the technique, but five years later I had succeeded in constructing a full-size casket, and shortly afterward I discovered how to mass-produce it in a way that would make it affordable. I succeeded in freeing people from the yoke of time. This was the greatest revolution in the history of mankind! Even the poorest could use the casket to wait for harvest time. This was what the world wanted, what the world needed. NO MORE FEBRUARYS!"

Cromwell had talked himself into a salesman's frenzy; he had obviously said this a thousand times before. He walked over to the window and stared in disbelief at the house on the other side of the street.

"That building is on the point of collapse. Is anybody inside it?"

"You should recognize the blue glow," Sigrun said. Cromwell stared at the house, but was distracted by a sleeping bat hanging from a curtain pole above him. He looked away and seemed to be thinking.

"Maybe Grace was on to something," he said after a while. "You do need a lot of wisdom to handle a thing like this."

"Give us the key," Sigrun said, "before it's too late."

"Come with me," said Cromwell. "There's something I have to show you."

He led them down a dark corridor. Out of habit, he flipped the light switch, but there was no power, so he found some candles to light their way. At the end of the corridor was a massive metal door; Cromwell spun the combination lock to open it, and showed them into a dark room where, through the fluttering light of the candles, they saw an ancient-looking casket in the middle of the floor. Cromwell went over to it and patted the lid.

"Isn't it beautiful?"

"Yes, it is beautiful," Sigrun said, "but I want to go home. I want to sit in the window with a friend and watch the rain. Now give me the key."

Cromwell looked at the children. There was a sad look in his eyes as he put his hand in his pocket, reciting a fragment of rhyme:

In a secret place
we found some space
for time and grace

There was a note of surrender in his voice as he handed them what looked like a gold credit card.

"This is the key. I won't be held responsible if something happens to you."

"Thanks," Sigrun said, taking it. They ran back home to Grace as fast as they could.

"Did you get the key?"

"Yes," said Marcus, "and also a little rhyme."

"Good," said Grace. "Let's go wake the world."

The Factory

Walking along the shore, the four children approached a huge factory that towered over the other buildings on the outskirts of the city. Large letters on its red-and-white towers spelled out the slogan:

TimeBox® – FOR BETTER TIMES!

They traversed a parking lot overgrown with heather and noticed how creepers had almost engulfed the gloomy building. The office wing was full of abandoned desks and yellowing papers. They walked over to a large factory building whose entrance was firmly closed by metal shutter doors. A tired-looking sign dangled from a screw: *Access strictly forbidden.*

Marcus switched on a screen next to the door. From a dusty speaker came a buzzing noise, and a mechanical voice said: *The key?*

Taking a deep breath, Marcus inserted the key card into the slot and recited the verse:

> *In a secret place*
> *we found some space*
> *for time and grace*

Open? prompted the screen. Marcus tapped *YES.*

Let time in? He shrugged and pressed *YES* again.

Are you wearing appropriate safety equipment?
Marcus looked at the others. "Yes or no?"

"Just say yes," said Kristin.

Are the feed containers full? Marcus looked over his shoulder.
"They must be. I mean—I don't know." Peter wasn't sure.
"Maybe Grace was deceiving us. Cromwell warned us against her.
This could be a trap."

"Feed containers for what?" Sigrun asked.

"I don't have a clue," Marcus said. He pressed YES. Slowly,
the shutter doors rolled open to reveal a space larger than any
sports stadium, with endless rows of white columns stretching
ahead as far as they could see. The ceiling was swathed in what
looked like white drapes.

"Wow!" said Sigrun, seizing Peter's hand.

"Silk drapes."

"But what now? What do we do next?"

"I've no idea," said Marcus. "Shall we go in?"

They moved into the vast, cathedral-like space; a magical light
flooded in through skylights, illuminating endless rows of black
and white columns, with rolls of silk stacked between them.

Kristin suddenly shrieked as a swarm of blowflies flew past.
She went across to the nearest column and saw masses of fat flies
pouring out of a pipe.

"Yuck! There's a tank here absolutely wriggling with maggots!"

A green-painted robot arm swung past just above their heads.
"This isn't silk," Marcus said. "It's spider webs!"

Now that their eyes had gotten used to the half-light, they
saw that what seemed to be a solid black column was in fact a
column crawling with spiders. The swarm of blowflies taking off
from the white column became caught in a web, and the black

column immediately came alive as the spiders set upon them; armies of spiders also lowered themselves from above so that the whole area seemed to be wriggling—the walls were moving, the columns pulsated, the ceilings were alive.

They gazed at the threads in amazement, and watched the big fat spiders spinning like crazy, deftly catching the flies, turning them into cocoons, and sucking the juice out of them.

"Let's go," Peter whispered, tugging at Sigrun. "The key must have restarted the factory. This place has been like one gigantic time casket."

Marcus stood frozen in his tracks. "I can't stand spiders!" Another green robot arm moved along the ceiling, rolling the spider webs into thick bolts of fabric that it dropped into a spinning frame. The robot moved back and forth like the shuttle of a gigantic loom, turning out stacks of large, black boards. A spider fell at their feet, and Kristin shrieked and stamped on it. It was hairy and huge, almost as big as her heel, and left a big green splat on the floor.

"Let's go," Marcus said. "It's a trap!"

All at once a gust of wind seemed to blow through the hall, the bolts of silk fell to the floor, blocking their exit, and all the spiders stopped spinning as one—as if they all simultaneously sensed fresh air. The emergency system started up and a red warning blinked over the entrance: *DOOR CLOSING! DOOR CLOSING! DOOR CLOSING!*

The spiders came floating down from the ceiling like special forces on ropes, cutting off their threads and covering the floor like a rising tide. They formed a thick layer that undulated like the sea, and the children clutched their faces and tried to protect themselves as spiders spattered them like ocean spray.

"Goddamn witch!" cried Marcus, trying to shake off spidery legs and antennae. "She's tricked us!"

Welcome to the World

The factory was completely quiet. The children cowered on the floor—Marcus hardly dared look up, but opened one eye and saw that all was clear aside from an occasional antenna or dead spider. With a low hum the robot arms continued shuttling back and forth collecting webs, but the spiders themselves were nowhere to be seen; though blowflies still hovered around, the scratching of antennae and spiders' legs was gone. The children ran out onto the parking lot and saw the swarm of spiders rippling across the land like a black shadow toward the city.

"Oh no! What have we done! They're going to attack the city!" Running after them, Marcus picked up a stick and managed to whack a few, but they were moving too fast. "Come on!" he yelled. "Help me!"

The others grabbed sticks too, but it was like trying to stop a forest fire with a broom handle. The black shadow covered the ground, and by now had gotten halfway into the city. But now another shadow appeared. The sky grew dark with crows flocking in from all directions; they swooped down, snatching spiders with their beaks and flying with them toward the town, where they released them to fall onto roofs and crawl down chimneys or through broken windows.

The children watched what was happening, paralyzed. "The animals have turned against the people," Kristin said, almost in tears. "Grace has betrayed us."

They ran as fast as they could and were huffing and puffing when they finally reached the first house. Crows sat cawing on the roof. The children peered through a broken parlor window and saw that the floor was covered with dandelions. Four spiders had attached themselves to a TimeBox in which a woman lay with a rigid smile, oblivious to what was happening.

Peter gripped his stick firmly. "Come on, we have to save her. We must kill the spiders!"

But Sigrun grabbed him and said: "No, hang on a moment..." The spiders sat calmly on the box and seemed to be munching at something. Suddenly there was a shrill noise like a microwave beeping, and a middle-aged woman stepped out of the box, looking dazed.

The children watched and giggled as the woman screamed at the sight of the spiders, but then fell silent as she contemplated the carpet of dandelions.

"Good afternoon," Marcus said.

"Good afternoon," said the woman. She was about to pick up the telephone, but it was covered with bird droppings.

"I don't like the look of things," she said, looking around. She picked up a remote control and tried repeatedly to switch the television on.

"What are you doing?" asked Sigrun.

"The government's obviously done nothing at all. I want to see what the economists have to say, whether the situation has gotten any better."

"Can't you see there's a blackbird's nest in the television?" Marcus said. With a sudden swish, four crows swept into the room, snatched up the spiders, and flew off with them, as the children watched in amazement.

"The spiders are chewing holes in the black boxes," Peter said.

253

"That's in their nature," Kristin said. "They eat their own webs, I learned about that in school."

"But my house has always been full of spiders," said Peter. "Why didn't they gobble up our boxes long ago?"

"This must be a different species. Each kind only eats its own web."

"It's almost as if somebody has trained the crows," said Kristin. "I wonder if anybody knows how to whisper a crow rhyme?"

The children ran to the next house and looked in. The same story repeated itself there, as a bewildered young man wearing polka-dot boxers emerged from his casket. A little toddler crawled out, and a woman in a bathrobe said to the man irritatedly: "Weren't you supposed to repaint the living room while I was in the box?"

She screamed and jumped onto a chair when she spotted the spiders, but the crows took them away before the man was able to squash them.

The children ran off again. "It seems like a tiny hole is enough to force the TimeBox open," Sigrun said, watching what was going on. They ran everywhere looking into homes and apartment buildings, and met people gazing fearfully at the crumbling world.

"It's okay! Don't be afraid. The world went off the rails. Now we need help to make things alright again. Come on!"

More and more people were coming out onto the streets. "Watch out for your kids!" Marcus yelled. "There are bears in the malls."

Peter was suddenly struck by an idea, and headed off to his friend Skyler's house; it no longer had a front door, so he went straight in and waited for the spiders to let time into Skyler's box.

"Hi. You back?" Skyler asked.

"Yeah, come out with me."

"I'm too old to play," he said in his deep voice, looking around. The room was full of pigeons.

"Nonsense," Peter said, dragging Skyler away, "of course you know how to play."

Main Street looked more or less like a circus, with a melee of small children, deer, seagulls, office workers, squirrels, and teenagers. A disoriented farmer was running behind his herd of cows on a grass-covered overpass.

"Wow, this is all so screwed up, what happened?" Skyler asked.

"I'll tell you later," said Peter with a grin.

"Everything will have to be rebuilt!"

"Yeah," said Peter, "but anything that's been built once can be built again."

Skyler scratched his head and thought that Peter was not all that stupid despite being just a kid.

"But perhaps some things should never have existed," said Peter, pointing at a bank building that looked like a gigantic, moss-covered tombstone.

They wandered together around the streets, chatting. People were astonishingly calm; some had already begun to clean up, while others drifted around as if they couldn't believe their own eyes. Skyler helped an old woman down a ladder and Peter looked after a young child for a man who was washing moss from the child's clothes. Skyler was enormously tall, but that soon ceased to feel strange to Peter: Skyler was still in there, even though he now inhabited an adult body.

"Skyler!" said Peter suddenly.

"Yeah?"

"We can still be friends, can't we, even if you're seven years older than me?"

"Yeah, I guess."

"When I'm seventy and you're seventy-seven, no one will notice anymore."

"Good point," Skyler said. They spotted the old guy from the toy store stretching a banner between a couple of trees.

WELCOME TO THE WORLD

He had more signs to put up, and Peter ran over to help him.

HAPPY TIMES AHEAD

Marcus heard a familiar voice calling his name, and saw his dad in the distance, running along the street and looking worried. Marcus jumped into his arms.

"Marcus, I was so worried about you!"

"No, I was the one who was worrying about you," said Marcus. "But everything's going to be alright now, we've got plenty of time."

"What happens now?"

"I don't know. Anything. Life goes on. Look at that sign there." His dad looked at the sign by the toy store.

EVERY DAY IS A GOOD DAY!

"It isn't quite as simple as that," he said, wrinkling his forehead.

"I know," said Marcus, "but since when has life been simple?"

His dad said nothing and put his arm around Marcus's shoulders.

*

Sigrun went home. She sat down on the living-room floor, looked at the frog on the coffee table, and waited. The crows were carrying spiders into a nearby neighborhood, but they hadn't reached her home yet. She could hear the growing excitement and commotion in the town as more and more people were released; children came running past, and someone farther down the street started playing a guitar.

Kristin came by. "Come with me! Let's go find Grace!"

"I can't, I'm waiting for Mom and Dad," said Sigrun.

"They won't notice anything! You'll only be a moment."

Sigrun tapped their boxes lightly and scribbled a note in case they should be set free while she was away: *Just popped out! Don't worry.*

They found their way back to the old house, but the couple that answered their knock didn't know anyone named Grace.

Beneath the Twisted Oak

F ar, far away, an old woman sat beneath a strangely twisted, ancient oak tree, holding a tattered note:

We will meet again!

Thanks to the crow rhyme, the birds were now flying all over the world, and she knew that everywhere time was flooding into people's boxes, filling their lives with joy and sorrow. At once generous and cruel, time would be playing around everybody like a fresh breeze, like a raging tempest, like a calm day. It would toughen people, lift them up to the heights, or blow them away like a grain of sand.

When the sun had set and stars were glittering in the endless night sky, she fell asleep on the softness of a mossy mound, canopied by the massive oak. In her dreams she saw dwarfs with eight legs, a sad king, and the beautiful Sunbeam gazing at her lovingly. She dreamed of three sisters who led her into a forest, where they chased stags and hares, antelopes and wild boars. But suddenly they stopped by a pair of small tree-shoots; one sister took her hand, another looked deep into her eyes, and the third whispered: *It's time.*

She woke when a soft, old hand stroked her cheek and a familiar voice chanted a verse in a language nobody but she could now understand:

Graceful as a swallow,
guileless as a lamb,
golden is her beauty—the whole world's charm.

She opened her eyes and found herself gazing into boyish eyes set in a weathered face.

"So tell me, Obsidiana, what's the news from the world of time?"